MYSTERY

A

W9-BVO-399

SILVER BIRD OF PREY

Large Print Lew
Lewis, Sheila.
Silver bird of prey

SILVER BIRD OF PREY

Sheila Lewis

Chivers Press • G.K. Hall & Co.
Bath, Avon, England   Thorndike, Maine USA

This Large Print edition is published by Chivers Press, England, and by G.K. Hall & Co., USA.

Published in 1997 in the U.K. by arrangement with Robert Hale Ltd.

Published in 1996 in the U.S. by arrangement with Robert Hale Ltd.

U.K. Hardcover ISBN 0–7451–4934–0 (Chivers Large Print)
U.S. Softcover ISBN 0–7838–1887–0 (Nightingale Collection Edition)

The text of this Large Print edition is unabridged.
Other aspects of the book may vary from the original edition.

Set in 16 pt. New Times Roman.

Printed in Great Britain on acid-free paper.

British Library Cataloguing in Publication Data available

Library of Congress Catalog Card Number: 96–94449

CHAPTER ONE

'And so, Gillian, I'm sorry to have to tell you, but you no longer have a job.'

Gillian Parker was gripped by panic at Mr Hunter's regretful words.

The small, rather overweight man she'd worked with for ten years drew his chair a little closer to her desk and leaned his arms heavily on the leather top, an anxious expression on his face.

'But, to tell you the truth, I'm really more worried about the men,' he said. 'You understand what I mean, my dear. They have families to support, while you have James to look after you.'

James! Gillian's heart leapt at the mention of his name. But she no longer had James. Of course, Mr Hunter didn't know that, she reminded herself. She'd never told him that James had walked out four months ago and she certainly couldn't tell him now. He had problems enough without hers.

'I'm so sorry about everything, really I am, Mr Hunter. Please don't worry about me, I'll be all right,' she lied, trying to force a smile.

'Do you want to go and speak to the men now?' she asked gently. It would be better for him to get it over as quickly as possible, she thought, perhaps lessening the strain on him at least a little.

'Do you think I should? It is a good idea, Gillian, you're right. Thank you.'

She almost wept at the gratitude in his sad eyes.

Despite her own situation, she grieved for Mr Hunter. The unstable heart condition, which was forcing him to close down his small central heating business, had been brought on by his hard work and endeavour to build it up.

Life's so unfair, she thought, then rejected that statement immediately. She'd always maintained that life was what you made of it. At least, that had been her philosophy until her own peaceful existence had literally fallen to pieces over the last few months. At that moment, Mr Hunter's return interrupted her thoughts.

'I hated doing that to them. They've been so reliable and trustworthy, and they took it so well.' He searched his pockets for a handkerchief. Gillian turned away so that she would not see his distress.

'It shouldn't be too difficult for them to find jobs.' She poured his tea, trying to cheer him up a little. 'Plumbers and electricians are always in demand. And the apprentices will probably stick with them.'

'Maybe,' he mumbled, almost lost in his depression.

'Hunter Heating has a marvellous reputation in Banford,' she went on

2

desperately. 'An automatic guarantee of high-quality workmanship.'

The sad eyes smiled at her for a moment.

'You've been a marvellous help all these years, Gillian. The firm wouldn't have made it without you.'

'Nonsense! Anyone could have done my job.' She smiled.

'And you, Gillian—will you take other employment or just stay at home and be a wife and—'

'Heavens, me at home? I'd go mad.' Her voice sounded shrill as she tried to hide the recurring panic behind a laughing facade.

'Nowhere else will be the same as Hunter's, though,' she managed to finish on a quiet note.

'You did something else before coming here, didn't you?'

She caught a sigh.

'Yes. I was in nursing.'

'Really? I'd have thought you were the ideal person for that. Why did you change horses in midstream, so to speak?'

Gillian hesitated for a moment.

'Sometimes I became a little too involved. Some cases could be distressing, but I've always wondered if I made a mistake. I always loved being on the children's wards.'

'Everyone will be on one month's redundancy pay, Gillian,' Mr Hunter broke in, 'but I've told the men to go out today and look for other jobs. We've only one contract to finish and we can do that by the end of next week. I'd like you to go home now, my dear. It's been a shock. I don't expect you to be here every day for the rest of the month. Talk things over with James and see what he thinks. I'm so glad you've got him.'

'You go home, too, Mr Hunter,' Gillian said quickly, the panic rising again. 'Your wife will be anxious about you.'

He managed a small smile, touched by her concern, and rose and walked to the door.

'You know, Gillian, if there's ever anything I can do for you, I mean after this'—he waved his hand around the small premises—'has all gone. Well, you know Grace and I ... you know we care. If you ever need a helping hand—well, you know where to find me.'

Gillian nodded, her throat too tight for words.

After he'd gone, she spent as long as possible tidying up her already-tidy desk, checking files and making out the redundancy slips. But the time came when she had to lock up and leave. There was nothing else to do.

She stood for a moment outside the office door and looked over the yard. A pale sun was striving to melt the unexpected spring frost that was glistening on the lengths of pipes, heap of old radiators, and the odds and ends that seemed to support the fence around the yard.

Jimmy and Ted, the plumbers, looked up as

4

Gillian walked across the yard.

'Bad do, isn't it, Gillian?' Jimmy, the senior, spoke first.

'It's very sad.' She shook her head.

'For the old chap, more than the rest of us,' put in Ted.

'Too true, we can find something else, but the old boy's got nothing left but memories,' Jimmy said slowly, 'albeit happy ones.'

Again Gillian felt tears threaten and briskly cleared her throat. 'Call in at the office on Monday and I'll give you the redundancy money.'

'No hurry, lass, we'll be around to the end, like yourself, eh?'

'Sure. I'll be here,' she said. 'Cheerio just now.'

She left them and walked over to her car. As she unlocked it, she reflected with a little bitterness that she would hang on to this job to the very end. How on earth was she going to face life otherwise?

*   *   *

Outside the yard, she turned into Banford's main through road. It didn't take her long to reach her own part of town. She could have walked, in fact, but the car was just another cocoon from the outside world.

The estate where she and James had lived for eight years still had a freshness about it that

5

was entirely due to the enthusiasm of the homemakers there.

'Heather Avenue is a caring road,' she used to say to James. 'You can tell by the sparkling houses and trim gardens, that we all care.'

Yes, she used to say that to James. When he was still around to hear it.

She parked well up her driveway, intending to slip into the house by the back door, but she didn't succeed. Sue Jackson next door was hanging out her washing.

'Gillian! Home already—not ill are you?'

Gillian paused. 'Flu-ish, I think.'

'Poor you. I'll pop in later and see if you need anything. Will James be home this week-end?'

'Shouldn't think so, but don't worry, I'll probably just sleep all the time,' Gillian tried to smile, then unlocked her back door and let herself into the house.

She flopped rather than sat on one of the kitchen chairs. She did feel awful, physically and mentally. Probably the effect of all those lies, she reflected ruefully.

She hoped she hadn't offended Sue. She was a super neighbour, reliable, but not pushing. Actually, she was rather special all round. A marvellous personality, out-going and confident, and always full of fun. All the things Gillian longed to be. For a moment, she wished she was more like Sue. She wouldn't have lied to the world, but would have had the courage, not only to tell the truth, but to face up to it.

She looked down at the bare white expanse of the kitchen table. It reminded her of the future. Endless, unmarked, and unrelieved. But that was self-pity, wasn't it? She could go on wallowing in it, if she liked, now that she had no job on top of everything else, or she could try to snap out of it.

The doorbell startled her.

'Electricity, madam. Meter, please.'

She showed the meter reader to the cupboard.

'Gone up quite a bit, Mrs Parker, what have you been doing—burning the midnight electricity? Never mind, maybe you'll win the pools.'

Gillian closed the door behind him, hoping the bill wouldn't be too high. She hated sending big bills to James. Maybe she could pay this one herself. But as she walked back into the kitchen it slowly, insidiously, dawned on her, that soon she would have no salary at all. Could she ask James to pay more then—for her car, too, for instance?

* * *

She began to wander round the rooms looking at the good carpets, heavy curtains, and solid furniture. Had she taken it all for granted? Now she was seeing everything with a startling clarity. True her own salary had helped to pay for many of the furnishings, but there was still

7

a mortgage and rates to be paid.

Could James be expected to carry on paying for those if she no longer contributed something? Of course he could—if he was coming back! But was he coming back?

Of course he was coming back. That was why she hadn't told anyone, not Mr Hunter, nor even Sue, that James had left her. It had been easy to say that this sales trip had been lengthened. James had travelled frequently, that's why she'd kept on her job.

But she hadn't heard from James at all in the past four months. She knew he paid the bills, and there was always sufficient money in their joint account for the housekeeping. Financially, he hadn't forgotten her. But otherwise?

Perhaps she was easy to forget. After all, he didn't seem to have thought much about her for a long time. It had come as a total shock when he'd told her there was someone else. Someone he'd known for a year and now they were so much in love, it wasn't fair of him to pretend to Gillian any longer.

She hadn't admitted it to herself, but she knew now that their life had drifted into a rut. Their weeks and week-ends became totally predictable, at least when James was at home. But still his news had paralysed her.

'I've known her for about a year, Gillian, she's—' James had begun.

'Don't tell me. I'm not interested.'

8

'You can't pretend she doesn't exist.'

'Tell me nothing about her,' she had insisted, too shocked to care any longer.

James tried to explain, but she had been unable to understand, or even try to comprehend. And then he'd gone. He'd made his choice—and it was this girl.

After she'd recovered from the initial shock, she reasoned it would be better to leave James alone, not to chase him, begging him to return, not to influence him in any way. Their marriage could only revive if he really wanted to return to her. But he must want to come back.

As surely he must! This girl was someone he'd met on his travels—in Harbury of all places, a small town some hundred odd miles from Banford.

Gillian could just imagine their affair. It must have been erratic to say the least. Sordid, in fact. Grabbing opportunities probably to be together when James was in that part of the country.

And James wasn't that type really. James was solid, respectable, unimaginative almost, the home-loving kind. Surely, he must have tired of her by now?

Quite suddenly, Gillian realised she had to know. She could no longer go on pretending that it would work out all right in the end, if she left matters alone.

She hadn't told anyone about James, she

9

realised now, because, basically, she didn't want to face things. She wanted her life to continue its meandering, peaceful way. A way forged out for her in the first place by her parents. A safe, secure childhood, then the venture into nursing which Dad had been worried about. When a bout of glandular fever had kept her at home for a couple of months, he'd talked her into giving up nursing and found her the office job with Mr Hunter. Night classes had given her a few skills in typing and book-keeping.

She hadn't been long with Mr Hunter when James, then salesman for a heating appliance company, had visited the office. Predictably, marriage had followed a pleasant, uneventful courtship.

Complacency had been her biggest fault, Gillian now realised. She had been complacent all her life because there had been a continual cushion for her to fall back on—her parents, James, and her job. Now, her parents were dead, James had gone and her job was no more. She had no one to rely on, but herself.

'Coo-ee—are you awake, Gillian?'

Sue's voice broke into her thoughts.

'In here, Sue.'

'How's the flu—oh—' Sue's eyes lost their concern and showed surprise at Gillian standing by the sideboard, pale instead of flushed.

'It isn't flu. I'm going away, probably for the

10

week-end,' Gillian said slowly.

'Oh. Fine. Good,' was all Sue would say. In that moment, Gillian knew that Sue had guessed—probably from the very beginning. She felt a warmth towards her neighbour, for her discretion and silent compassion. Sue would never ask any awkward questions.

'Will you keep a key for me? I'll be back Monday at the latest.'

'Of course I will.' Sue smiled, then paused. 'You know ... you can rely on me.'

Gillian knew she could unload all her troubles on to Sue's shoulders if she wanted to. But, for once, she'd try to sort this mess out herself.

'Thanks. But I have to do it this way, otherwise I'll be back to square one. Sorry, I'm not making much sense.'

'I think I understand what you're not saying, love. Anyway, you know where to find me ... that's corny, too.' She came over and grasped Gillian's arm. 'I hope it turns out ... the way you want it to. Take care.'

She left as quickly as she'd come.

One day she'd tell Sue just how much she'd helped. Not until she had come, had Gillian thought of going to see James, but the very positiveness of Sue's action after her earlier promise, somehow pointed the way. When Sue said she would do something, she did.

She had to change. She had to shed her complacency, which was a negative attitude,

11

after all. She fetched the slip of paper with James's address from the telephone table.

'*Eidelweiss, Greenwood Lane, Harbury,*' and a telephone number was all that was written on it.

She could ring James, of course, but that was the easy way, the old Gillian's way. Now, she had to act. Putting the address into her handbag, she walked briskly into their bedroom, her mind clear and decisive, as if all the cobwebs of the last four months, and longer, had been swept clean away.

The wardrobe open, she surveyed her clothes. It was important to wear just the right outfit. No, not the old cliché outfit—'my husband's favourite,' nor the equally predictable one of something new and startling to impress.

Although she tried on a few outfits, Gillian knew as soon as she took the green two-piece from its hanger, that she'd been going to wear this all along. It flattered her slim waist, suggested added height to her five feet three inches, and brought out the shy auburn tints in her brown hair.

It also gave her much needed confidence. No, the old Gillian was not quite discarded yet, it seemed.

Since Harbury was too far away to make the round trip in one day, she packed an overnight bag. It was noon already, anyway. Soon she had locked up, passed the key over the fence to

12

Sue and stowed her suitcase in the back of the car.

'Hope the little green monster doesn't let you down,' Sue called.

Gillian shook her head, in mock despair. The car was rather elderly and spare parts were difficult to find for the out-of-date model. But the engine leapt to life at the first touch. Gillian waved to Sue and drove out of Heather Avenue, remembering the day when she'd brought the car home after it had been re-sprayed bright green, mistakenly, and James had promptly dubbed it the Monster from Mars.

Involuntarily, she smiled at the memory. Those were the good days. She turned off the main road into the Heather Lane petrol station, still thinking of James, still thinking she couldn't really remember any bad days. Except the last one.

'Morning, Mrs Parker. Usual?' The petrol station attendant, with a mop of carroty permed hair, grinned in greeting.

'Hello, Eric. No ... I'll need her filled up to the top. Going on a bit of a journey,' she told him.

'I'll check the old tyres as well then. Did you remember to check the oil before you started her this morning?'

'No ... I forgot,' She could hardly tell him that she had only planned this trip in the last half hour.

13

'Never mind. You've been pretty regular in checking it. I expect it will be O K.'

Gillian gave him a helpless smile. Until James had gone, he'd done everything for her, like checking her car, and so details like oil and tyres had never crossed her mind. Like everything else in life, she'd just accepted that things would run smoothly forever.

Over the last few months, she'd made an effort to see that the car was run efficiently and Eric had cheerfully advised her on most things.

'Going far?'

'Up north. To see some ... old friends.'

'Motorway it is then. I'll put a spare fan belt in the boot.'

Preparations completed, she went on her way.

*　　*　　*

Stopping at a service station she had some coffee and a salad sandwich. Perhaps she ought not to stop again as she wanted to reach Harbury before dark. She bought a bar of chocolate and some fruit which she could have later in the afternoon.

After an hour or so, Gillian stopped in a lay-by. She got out of the car and, taking some chocolate and an apple, went over to sit on a low, stone wall. The air was pure magic—fresh, yet catching her throat, so she had to take deep breaths.

14

Maybe it was the countryside up here that had attracted James. Maybe, instead of just holidaying here, he wanted to live here. But that theory didn't really hold water, Gillian realised. It wasn't as if he'd asked her to move up here. No, he'd not wanted her here.

She stuffed the apple core and chocolate wrapper in her bag and went back to the car. On the outskirts of Harbury, she stopped at a service station. The little green monster had done well so far, but needed more petrol—and she needed a little more time before seeing James. Her thoughts, as she waited inevitably returned to James and their eight-year marriage.

The only thing the marriage had seemed to lack was children. Gillian had hoped and hoped, but she'd never become pregnant. There had been no medical reason why they shouldn't have children. Perhaps now—when they got together again?

'That's it, miss—'

'Oh, thanks.' Gillian paid the attendant. 'Perhaps you can help me.' She fished James's address out of her handbag. 'Greenwood Lane—is it far?'

'Right on the other side of town, miss. Best to take the by-pass. Keep right on it till you think you're back in the wilds, but then you'll see the turning on your left.'

'Thanks a lot.'

After a particular bumpy journey, Gillian

15

was faced by a large sign. 'Eidelweiss Hotel. Licensed, dinner dances Fridays and Saturdays, Folk Club Sundays.'

She braked abruptly. Beside the hotel sign was another—'No Through Road.'

A hotel! James must be living there. She felt her heart lift a little. He couldn't be living with her then—not in a hotel. Maybe everything would be all right after all. Perhaps he had been waiting for Gillian to make the first move.

Right, she was here. So, what next? She'd very deliberately not thought out this next move on the long journey, because she knew if she went over all the implications, she might turn tail. But things looked better now. It was more than likely that she wouldn't have to .meet the girl at all. She glanced at her watch. Five-thirty. Bit early perhaps for James. She looked around. No sign of his car. Still, she could go into the bar and have a drink while waiting.

Gillian slowly approached the reception desk, noticing that the showcases had cleverly-arranged displays of antique jewellery in one, and miniatures and silhouettes in the Victorian-style in the other. Each case had a small, gold embossed card lying on the velvet lining, reading simply—'Skua Antiques.'

'I'm so sorry, I didn't hear you come in. I won't be a moment. If I lose my place now, I'll never find this particular Jones again!' The receptionist smiled.

16

Gillian smiled. 'Please—I'm in no hurry.'

The girl was pleasant-looking and dressed in a simple, yet beautifully-cut, floral-printed top. It had a tie neckline and this was fastened with a heavy antique silver brooch, designed in the shape of an unusual bird. It occurred to Gillian that the girl obviously patronised 'Skua Antiques.'

As she looked away, her eye caught sight of a name plaque on the desk. It said, 'Receptionist: Miss Barbara Reynolds.'

Miss Reynolds picked up the card index box and slipped it beneath the counter.

'There, thanks for being so patient.' Brown eyes, a match for her smock smiled at Gillian. 'Now, how may I help you?'

'Well, I wondered—is—could I see,' Gillian floundered for a moment, then got a grip on herself. 'I'm sorry. I wanted to see Mr James Parker.'

There was a perceptible pause.

'Mr Parker isn't here at the moment. I could take a message. Will you leave your name, please?'

'No, no—what time did you say he'd be here?'

'I didn't. Do you have business with him?'

Gillian's arm was jostled.

'Excuse me, please.'

She turned. A small, plump, cheerful lady beamed at her, proferring her key to the receptionist at the same time.

17

'Thanks, Barbara, I'll be back at eight in time for dinner,' she turned back to Gillian. 'If I take my key with me, I'll lose it, bound to. 'Bye for now.'

Quickly, Gillian turned back to the desk. 'Well, yes, I do have business with him in a way. It's urgent too. I must see Mr Parker tonight.'

The brown eyes of Miss Reynolds were no longer smiling. In fact, they were a little frosty.

'I'm Gillian Parker,' she said firmly.

'His wife?' The words escaped the receptionist's lips, quickly and quietly.

Gillian, aware that a fair girl was still hovering by the dining-room entrance, replied equally quietly. 'Yes.'

'Mr Parker is away at the moment,' the receptionist said briefly.

She felt quite deflated. All this way and James must be away on yet another business trip. She should have telephoned. So much for decisiveness.

'Oh—when will he be back?'

'When he has recovered.'

'Recovered?' Two sensations registered with Gillian simultaneously. Fear, that something was wrong with James and surprise at the hostility in the receptionist's voice.

'He's been ill?'

'Yes, Mrs Parker. Pleurisy with complications.'

A flood of panic and worry and something

18

else, washed over Gillian. She looked around again.

'Look—I didn't know about this—have you an office where we could talk?'

There was a longer pause from the girl behind the desk, then she said, 'I'm sorry. I can't leave reception. There's no one else to take my place.'

Gillian fiddled with her bag for a moment. She would just have to find out what she could about James right here.

'Is he in hospital?'

'Not any longer. Excuse me, please.' Barbara Reynolds looked over Gillian's shoulder.

'Yes, Mr Johnston?'

'Will I get a bus about eight tonight from the lane end, Miss Reynolds?' a deep voice spoke from behind Gillian.

'That's right. And the last one leaves Harbury at eleven-fifteen, Mr Johnston.'

'Thank you, Miss Reynolds. Won't be too late to order cocoa when I come in?'

'Of course not. Enjoy your evening, Mr Johnston.'

Gillian heard the conversation without registering it. Her mind was confused. James ill and she'd never known. Why?

'Didn't my husband ask someone to inform me he was ill?' she asked.

'He thought it best not to—to upset you.'

It was an ordinary enough remark, and one

19

that Gillian would have accepted, but for the look of defiance in Barbara Reynolds' eyes.

* * *

This was James's girl. It was as clear as if she'd shouted the information at Gillian. She stood transfixed, staring at Barbara Reynolds, unaware that it was pure shock that prevented her from speaking, turning away, or even disengaging her eyes from the girl's defiant, but slightly wary stare.

She was only just aware that Barbara Reynolds knew she'd guessed the truth.

'Of course, had you telephoned, I would have told you.'

It was there again, the accusatory tone.

'Four months is a long time. Didn't you wonder how he was?' the girl continued.

'He hasn't inquired about me in that time either.' Hurt and shock made Gillian reply sharply.

'But he has heard from you. Bills for instance. He knew your life was going on as usual.'

Oh, that was unfair. James had walked out on her, not the other way around, Gillian's senses screamed silently.

'I—' She paused. She was in a public place. People were coming and going from the bar and the dining-room. Nobody seemed to be paying any attention, but she didn't want a

20

public argument.

'Where is James?' she asked quietly.

'Recuperating in the Lake District. Taking some hill walks to recover his strength.'

'When does he plan to return?'

'When he is well,' Barbara Reynolds said flatly.

She was giving nothing away, thought Gillian bitterly. And she's more than a match for me.

Yet there was a quiet dignity about the girl, Gillian reluctantly admitted. She was obviously not an opportunist, as she had previously surmised. This was no cheap adventure between James and her. Did she love him? Did he love her? Enough to put aside eight years of marriage Gillian found herself wondering.

She realised, too, that most of Barbara Reynolds' hostile attitude might have its origins in guilt. She was obviously decent enough not to relish the position of the 'other woman.'

'Perhaps you would be good enough to tell him I came to see him and that I'd like to talk with him,' Gillian said without fuss.

The girl's attitude changed perceptibly, probably because she realised Gillian was not going to make a scene.

'I'll tell him. Shall I ask him to telephone you?'

'Yes.'

21

For a moment they looked squarely at each other. She might even be my age, thought Gillian. It isn't even a case of a younger girl. She hadn't that challenge to fight. Maybe it was something that James had become involved in and didn't know how to end. Perhaps when he realised Gillian still loved him, he'd give up Barbara.

Gillian turned away slowly and walked towards the entrance door, thinking she wanted James back—but fairly. No emotional blackmail. She was about to pull open the door when she remembered about her redundancy. If he knew about that, he might think she only wanted him back for financial support. Perhaps she'd better tell Barbara Reynolds that James shouldn't ring her at Hunter's, only at home. That way he wouldn't find out until later. Yes, that was the best idea.

She turned round, but couldn't see Barbara Reynolds at first. The fair girl who'd been loitering outside the dining-room was coming over to the main door. Briefly, Gillian wondered if she'd heard their conversation. Oh, well, it couldn't be helped.

And then she saw Barbara. She'd left the reception desk and was on her way to the dining-room. Suddenly, she became aware that Gillian was still in the hotel and staring at her.

Barbara flushed scarlet, but Gillian wasn't looking at her face. She was looking at the fine floral smock which floated around the girl, not quite successfully hiding the fact that she was pregnant.

Gillian whirled round and wrenched open the entrance door. Not caring who saw her, she ran across the forecourt to her car. Her fingers fumbled with the key, but finally she unlocked the door and almost threw herself inside.

Faintly, she thought she heard someone calling, 'Mrs Parker,' but she jammed the key in the ignition. The engine spluttered and died twice, but the third time it fired. She threw the gear into reverse and looked over her shoulder. There was no one about. Quickly she turned the car and raced down the hotel's winding driveway, her head, shoulders, and arms tight with tension.

No wonder James hadn't contacted her. How could he? He could hardly leave Barbara Reynolds, if she was expecting his child! A sob caught in Gillian's throat. She'd never expected this. Never. Had she lost James forever? Oh no, surely not, not like this. A child. They'd always wanted a child, but somehow it had been denied them. Now, another woman was expecting his child.

Hardly aware where she was going, the sharp bend into Greenwood Lane was upon her before she realised it. She braked automatically and changed down a gear, but she was still going quite fast and suddenly the delicately shadowed road of the afternoon was dark and gloomy in the fast approaching dusk.

Even as she tried to adjust her eyes and speed to the gloom, she was conscious of a pale figure running out from between the trees on her left. Her foot came down on the brake. Surely the person could see her? But the figure hurtled over the road right in front of her.

Gillian swerved, pulling the wheel over as hard as she could, knowing she'd never stop in time.

It was too late. There was a dull thud as her front wing caught the running figure and she saw the solid shape of a tree right in front of her. Her foot had pressed the brake to the floor, but there was total impact and the quiet dusk was violated by the shriek of rending metal and smashing glass.

CHAPTER TWO

For a moment, life itself seemed suspended.

But then Gillian gradually became aware that she could see, hear and move.

She realised the front of her car had been badly dented in the collision with the tree. There was a throbbing ache in her arm, too, which had somehow come between her chest and the steering-wheel, no doubt preventing more serious injury. Then, with sudden horror, she remembered the cause of the accident—the figure in white—the running figure, hit by her car. Who was it? And where had it come from?

Careless of her painful arm, Gillian struggled to get out of her car. There, a few feet from her, lay a girl wearing pale-blue slacks and a T-shirt.

She knelt beside the girl, panic and concern returning. What had made her run out like that right in front of her car, which she must have seen? As Gillian touched her, she opened her eyes, pale-blue and child-like.

'Are you hurt?' Gillian asked urgently.

'No, no, I don't think so.' The girl tried to sit up and Gillian quickly slipped a supporting arm round her.

Gillian remembered her now. She was the same girl who had been in the Eidelweiss Hotel all the time she was talking with Barbara Reynolds.

'You came out of the trees so fast. Didn't you see me?' she asked her gently.

The girl's eyes filled with tears. 'Please, help me. You can help me,' she grasped Gillian's arm tightly.

'Of course I will. I'll call someone from the hotel—'

'No, no!' the girl seemed to panic. 'Not from there.' She paused and looked towards the trees. Gillian had heard sounds, too. Someone was moving quickly and noisily through the woods.

As Gillian assisted the girl to her feet, she clung on tightly. 'Promise that you'll help me.

Please!'

By the strong pressure of the girl's fingers on her arm, Gillian knew she wasn't badly injured, but perhaps dazed by shock, pleading like this.

'I promise,' she said placatingly.

The worry disappeared like magic from the baby-blue eyes and the girl managed a small smile.

'Holly!'

Both girls turned at the sound of the strong shout. A tall, broadly-set man appeared through the trees opposite to the hotel entrance road, and in three short strides he was by the girl's side, taking in her dishevelled appearance and shaky stance.

'I heard a crash—have you been hurt?' His glance darted quickly in the direction of Gillian's crumpled car.

'She didn't see me,' Holly announced. 'She doesn't know the road and you know how dark the trees make it.'

Gillian opened her mouth to protest. This girl was implying that it was her fault! But, before she could speak, the man turned hard, accusing eyes on her.

Gillian found she was trembling and aching at the same time under his gaze. Had the girl meant to run out in front of her car and didn't want this man to know? She felt too shaken to puzzle it out.

'I'm sorry—' she began, but he gave her only a scathing glance and turned back to the girl.

'At least you don't seem too badly hurt.' Gently, he assisted her to rest against the car's battered bonnet. 'Come on, lean on me, Holly.'

'Can—can I help?' Gillian stammered.

'I'm going to take my sister home. I think you'd better get help as regards your car,' he replied. 'You're not hurt, I take it?'

She shook her head.

'Please, Roy. I want Gillian to come with us. She said she would help me,' the girl said, giving Gillian a beseeching look.

'Yes, I did promise.' She took Holly's other arm.

Giving Gillian a cursory glance, he turned his attention to her car.

'Your car is no danger to anyone for the moment since it is right off the road,' he said dryly. 'I suppose you'd better come home with us. You can telephone a garage from the cottage. This way.' He gestured through the trees. Supporting Holly, they set off on a narrow, but well-beaten path through the dim woods.

'This is my brother, Roy Andrews,' the girl said. 'I'm Holly. Roy, this is Gillian.'

Roy Andrews grunted an acknowledgement.

Gillian said, 'Hello,' perfunctorily wondering how Holly knew her name.

'Were you at the Eidelweiss again, Holly?' Her brother's voice was tight with disapproval.

'Heavens, no. I popped into Harbury for

27

some odds and ends and decided to walk back. You know I enjoy the fresh air,' she finished on a plaintive note.

The ache in Gillian's head developed into a steady throb. She didn't like the way this conversation was going. She'd just see this girl home and then return to her car, which she hoped wasn't too badly damaged. There was really no hope of returning home to Banford tonight, but she might find a hotel room somewhere in Harbury.

They approached Roy Andrews' cottage from the rear. Built with local stone, it had mellowed with the years, but the peeling paint on the window frames and the blistered and bleached back door gave it a run-down appearance.

Roy led them through a stone-flagged passageway from the back door into a well-proportioned lounge. A comfortable looking sofa and lived-in armchairs dominated the room, but in a brief glance round Gillian noticed there were also some good pieces of furniture.

But she only wanted to sit down on the sofa beside Holly.

Holly dropped her head and covered her eyes with her hands. Gillian was horrified to realise that she was crying.

'Shock,' Roy Andrews said tersely. 'Holly, I'm calling Dr Miller. You need a check-up. Excuse me.' He nodded to Gillian and left the room.

Gillian bent down. 'Let me take your shoes off, Holly, then you can lie on the sofa.'

'Thanks, you are really helping, Gillian.'

Gillian looked at her sceptically. In what way? By lying and taking the blame for the accident? She hadn't expected that to be the 'help' she promised to give.

'You don't look very well yourself,' Holly said.

'Just a bit shaken, that's all,' Gillian replied. 'A good night's sleep will work wonders.' It was safer to stick to old cliches, not to express her real feelings. 'Anyway, I must be off soon.'

'No—no, don't leave—' Holly broke off as her brother came in carrying a tray with mugs of tea.

'Dr Miller will be here directly,' he said, sweeping aside some magazines from a coffee table. 'Harbury Garage are on their way to look at your car.' He nodded in Gillian's direction.

As she sipped her tea, her eye caught two paintings on the wall. Even to her untutored eye, she knew they were good. She became aware, too, of expensive ornaments about the room, mostly silver. But for all that, there was an air to the cottage, and its garden, of neglect. With sudden insight, Gillian realised it all lacked a woman's touch.

'That'll be the doctor. You'd better go up to

your room,' Roy said to Holly as they heard the sound of a car arriving.

* * *

Gillian had tidied the tea things on the tray, collected her handbag, and was standing, ready to leave, when Roy Andrews came back into the living-room.

'Thank you for the tea, Mr Andrews, and I really am sorry about the accident,' she said.

'Coming from the hotel, were you?'

'Yes,' Gillian said, surprised, then read the expression in his eyes. 'I hadn't been drinking.'

He lifted his hands in a gesture of apology.

'I didn't see your sister until—'

'Until it was too late. However, I noticed from the car tracks that you did swerve to avoid her.'

'Of course!'

'It may take some time to repair your car. Would you like to telephone anyone—your husband, perhaps?'

'No—no, it's all right thank you.'

'You don't live in Harbury, do you?'

'No, Banford.'

Roy Andrews raised his eyebrows. 'You are a long way from home. Visiting friends here?'

'Yes and no,' Gillian stammered.

'Which is it?'

'I came to see someone at the Eidelweiss, but he isn't there.'

'And were you intending to go back to

Banford tonight?'

'I didn't know.'

'Do you mean to say you drove all this way, not knowing whether you would stay or not?' His tone was derogatory, his suspicions obvious. 'Sorry, it's none of my business,' he added almost as an afterthought.

It was patently obvious to Gillian that he thought she'd come to Harbury on some clandestine affair. The irony of it!

'I came to visit my husband.'

'Is he staying at the Eidelweiss?'

'Yes, he's been staying there for—for a while.' She knew it wouldn't make any sense to him, but that was as far as she was prepared to go. She didn't see any reason to tell him any more.

'I see.' He paused for a moment. 'So obviously, you were upset when you left the hotel. That would account for the fact that you didn't see my sister.'

'I did see your sister, Mr Andrews. But I had no chance!'

His eyes opened wide at the insistence in her tone but, mercifully, the doctor came into the room before he could question her further.

'Holly is fine, Roy. Just a few bruises and a bit of a shake. I've given her something to ensure a good night's rest. See that she takes it easy for a day or two.' He turned to Gillian. 'I take it you must be her friend. She asked if you'd go up to her.'

31

'Oh, but I was just leaving.'

'Just for a few moments. I think it would help her,' the doctor said with smooth professional insistence.

Gillian knew Roy Andrews was watching her closely. She wanted nothing more than to get away from here, to get away from people. She'd had enough of problems today. She wanted to retreat into herself, but obviously this was not to be.

'Surely.' She smiled briefly.

As she passed the doctor, he raised his hand to detain her.

'You are all right, I take it?' he said kindly.

'Oh, I'm fine,' she lied.

'Second room on the right at the top of the stairs,' Roy Andrews said.

Holly was almost asleep when Gillian reached her bedroom. She smiled weakly.

'You've been a real friend today, Gillian, and I do desperately need someone to talk to. Tell Roy I said you have to stay. You know you can't go anywhere tonight, anyway,' she finished with quiet triumph.

But Gillian didn't pass on her message. Roy Andrews was speaking on the telephone when she left the bedroom.

'... I see, let me know the position tomorrow, please.'

Gillian stood awkwardly in the hall, anxious to leave.

'That was the garage,' he said replacing the

32

receiver. 'They've had to tow your car away. They won't be able to assess the extent of the damage until tomorrow.'

'Oh, no! But I must go.' In panic, she turned abruptly. 'I can catch a bus from the lane, can't I? I'll have to go and inform the police in Harbury.'

'Don't rush away to the bus, I'll take you in the car.' Roy reached out to take her arm and Gillian gasped in pain. He caught her as she swayed a little.

'Hold on, you have been hurt! Why didn't you tell Dr Miller?'

'I didn't want to make a fuss.'

Firmly, but gently, he led her back to the living-room.

'Sit down,' he said gently.

'You'd better stay here tonight,' he said with finality.

'No—I couldn't impose.'

'Look Gillian whatever-your-name-is. You have no car. You can't drive, anyway, because of your arm, and your husband is goodness knows where. What else are you going to do?'

She obviously had no choice.

*   *   *

When she woke the following morning, Gillian felt much better, but this was entirely due to medication.

There was no way she would have even

33

closed an eye after the events of yesterday, if Roy Andrews hadn't insisted on her taking two of the sleeping pills which the doctor had left for Holly.

Sleep would have been impossible after that ghastly talk with Barbara Reynolds, the girl James had left her for. She still hadn't seen James, didn't even know when she would, and now that she knew Barbara was pregnant, she had to realise that perhaps she and James were totally finished.

And then Holly and the accident. Gillian realised that Holly must have been eavesdropping on her conversation with Barbara. How else would she have known her name?

Gillian knew, too, that Roy Andrews blamed her entirely for the accident, although he'd said nothing about that when the police had called for details last night.

She was just about to get out of bed when she became aware of the bedroom door opening slowly and silently, but no one appeared.

'Come in,' she called, hastily snatching up Holly's wrap from the bottom of the bed.

To her amazement, a child appeared, a boy of about nine. He was carrying a tray, with a mug, sugar basin, and cream jug. He kept his head down, concentrating on not spilling the tea. All Gillian could see was a mop of fair, unruly hair. He deposited the tray on a bedside table and stood, still not looking up.

Gillian, a childhood sufferer from intense shyness, recognised his problem right away.

'Thank you so much. I really ought to have been up by now.' She tried to sound cheerful, as if she was used to looking only at the tops of people's heads.

'I'm Gillian,' she said casually, as she stirred her tea, but still there was no reply, or movement from the child.

'Mmm, this tea is heaven. Did you make it?'

For an instant, he lifted his head, looked at her, then nodded vigorously, his eyes studying the floor once again.

But in that flashing look, she'd seen the Andrews eyes. Blue and clear—not pale and indecisive like Holly's nor yet with that cold maturity of her brother's, but clear and honest.

'Is it a nice day?' She leaned over and pulled back one curtain. The boy darted forward and pulled the other.

'Is that your dog outside?' She pointed through the window.

Another flashing look and a nod.

'What's his name?'

Silence.

'Hasn't he got one?'

A shake of the head.

'Gosh, we'll have to think up one for him. Tell you what, I'll get dressed and when I come downstairs maybe we can talk about it.' Before she'd finished speaking, the boy had snatched up the tray and fled the bedroom.

Gillian sat on the bed for a moment. Poor lad, so desperately shy. Was he a younger brother to Roy and Holly, she wondered?

Roy Andrews was alone in the kitchen when she went down.

'Thank you for the tea. I really meant to be down earlier. I think the pills knocked me out,' she told him.

'The best thing for you. I was so worried about Holly that I didn't realise you must be shaken, too,' he said off-handedly. 'Did Chris manage to bring the tea without spilling it?'

'Yes. Not a drop was missing. Is he your young brother?'

'He's my son.'

Gillian looked out of the kitchen window. The boy was in the bare garden playing with the dog. A dog of unknown parentage, but an endearing mixture of long ears, ridiculous tail, and sleek long hair. It looked like a good game between them, but it was quiet—totally quiet. No shouts, yells, or even barks.

'How is Holly this morning?' Gillian asked, still puzzling over the boy's silence.

'A bit stiff and sore, but I think she'll be all right. I've told her to stay in bed.'

Gillian looked at the cluttered and untidy kitchen. Certainly, Roy Andrews couldn't cope with this alone.

'Can I help with anything? Take up breakfast to Holly for instance?'

'She never eats breakfast. I've made some

36

sausage and egg. Do you mind having it in here?' he said.

'Of course not.' Gillian sat down in the chair he indicated.

He opened the kitchen window. 'Breakfast, Chris.'

When the boy came in, he slid into a chair, not looking at, or speaking to, anyone. Once again, Gillian was surprised by Roy Andrews. Although he exchanged no words with his son, there was gentleness and love in the simple way he served and watched the boy.

Gillian ate the dried sausage and curled egg as best she could. It was obviously normal fare for Roy and his son.

'Have you thought of a name yet?' she said conversationally to the boy.

He shook his head again, but Gillian noticed the sideways glance he gave his father.

'How about Thumper—after his tail?' she suggested.

The blue eyes flashed at her again, but there was also a look of uncertainty on his face. Then the head went down again, nodding.

Gillian was aware of Roy Andrews looking at her closely. She wondered if she'd been interfering, perhaps there was a family name for the dog after all.

'May I telephone the garage to see if my car is ready?' she asked, a little confused.

'I'll take you there. I have to pick up some shopping anyway.'

37

Suddenly, the boy slid out from his seat and made for the kitchen door.

'Goodbye,' Gillian called.

The back door was wrenched open and the boy would have gone but for his father's cry.

'Chris!'

The child turned, looked briefly at Gillian and raised a hand in farewell. His father said nothing.

Gillian sat there, immobile. Was the child unable to talk at all? Had she made some terrible mistake in trying to converse with him? She realised now, his father had never asked him anything that required an answer during the whole meal.

She turned to find Roy watching her.

'He can speak, but he won't,' he said quietly. 'It's shock, according to Dr Miller. He's been like that since his mother died last year—in a car accident.'

Roy Andrews rose from the table, but not before Gillian had seen the anguish in his eyes.

She took the dishes to the sink and began washing up automatically, glad to have something to keep her hands busy while her thoughts were so disturbed. No wonder Roy Andrews had been so upset at yesterday's accident. It must have revived very painful memories.

'You don't need to do that,' his voice said behind her.

'I'd like to help,' she replied simply.

'Perhaps you'd take this cup of coffee up to Holly, then.'

*   *   *

Holly was sitting up in bed, looking fragile and wan.

'Are you all right, Gillian?' she asked. 'Roy said you'd hurt your arm.'

'Yes, I'm fine now. I had a good sleep and I'm just about ready to go.'

The large baby-blue eyes widened. 'Oh, no, please, Gillian, don't go. You promised to stay. You know you did.'

'I promised to help, Holly and I did—last night. But now I have to get back to my life—and leave you to yours.'

Holly looked at her thoughtfully.

'You've met Chris?'

'Yes.'

'It's sad, isn't it? If only he could talk to someone, I know it would all come out fine. And it's killing Roy too. He adores Chris. But he can't get near him like this.' She examined her hands. 'There's just the three of us here and it's not exactly a cosy, happy home.'

Roy Andrews came into the bedroom and looked at Gillian.

'That was the garage on the phone. Your car isn't going to be ready for some time, a few days, perhaps.'

'Oh, no! I'll have to go home by train.'

39

'You can't go, Gillian.' Holly sat up in bed urgently. 'Tell her she can stay here, Roy.'

'But she can't,' he answered bluntly.

'She can't go back, Roy! Her husband left her, you know, and she's trying to find him here in Harbury.'

Gillian only just managed to contain her gasp of shock. How could Holly! But she saw Roy looking at her again with that odd mixture of thoughtfulness and compassion.

'And anyway,' Holly continued. 'I can't possibly get up for a day or two. If Gillian stayed to help out, it would make her feel much better about the accident!'

'Holly, that's uncalled for!' Roy said at once.

'Where can she stay then? The only decent hotel here is the Eidelweiss and she won't stay there!'

'Please—I'll go home to Banford,' Gillian tried to make herself heard.

Roy held up his hand. 'O K. Holly, I agree, she can stay,' he said, then wearily turned to Gillian. 'You'll never find a place to stay in Harbury. Besides, if you look after my sister, you will earn your keep and more!' he turned and walked out of the room.

'Well, you'll never have a more ungracious invitation than that, but promise you'll stay, Gillian. I know we can be friends!'

Gillian moved over to the window. She really didn't feel like going all the way home to Banford with the situation between her and

40

James unresolved. It would take tremendous courage to come back here again to face Barbara Reynolds.

It might not be easy to stay here, but at least she would be able to help. Today was Saturday, and she would probably have the car back by Monday. She could telephone Mr Hunter and tell him she would be a day late in returning to the office. It didn't matter now that the firm was closing down. And James might return from his holiday this week-end.

She turned to Holly. 'I'd better get my overnight bag from my car.'

'Oh, good.' Holly clapped her hands.

Downstairs, she mentioned her bag to Roy and asked if she could fetch any shopping while she was in Harbury.

'I have to go into town myself. We'll take the car and do both things at once,' he said.

As they walked out to the car, Gillian saw Chris standing very still and knew he was covertly watching them.

'We're going into town to do some shopping. Don't go far. Holly is still in bed,' Roy called to him.

Chris watched as his father reversed the car, his expression unreadable.

'Would he like to come with us?' Gillian asked Roy.

'Coming?' Roy called through the open car window.

But the boy turned and ran into the cottage.

41

Roy's face was very carefully composed, although Gillian sensed he was bitterly disappointed by Chris's reaction.

* * *

They did the shopping and collected her overnight bag with an economy of time and words between them. Gillian found her car had been towed to the garage where she'd picked up petrol the previous day.

'It's a bit on the elderly side, miss.' The mechanic patted the little green monster. 'Spare parts for this foreign job are hard to come by.'

'Oh, dear, I need it so desperately too,' she told him.

'Don't worry, love, I've got my connections.' He tapped his large nose and winked.

'You'll give me a ring as soon as it's ready,' Roy Andrews said.

'Will do, Mr Andrews.'

When they got back to the cottage, Gillian set about cleaning up, trying to do it in such a way that it would not offend Roy. He'd more than enough strain to cope with already, she reckoned.

All the time Gillian was aware of Chris hovering around, not too near, yet not too far, rather like a shadow moving with the sun. She was careful not to make a fuss of him, or to

42

encourage him to try speaking. She knew his shock was too deep-seated for that. She treated him with naturalness although she found she was strangely drawn to him and sensed it was reciprocated. There was an unspoken rapport between them.

Holly had no objections to staying in bed and being waited on by Gillian. Despite her bruises, she was cheerful and only seemed to lose her bounce when Gillian mentioned leaving.

'Don't go, Gillian, please stay.' Her distress seemed genuine.

On the Sunday evening, Gillian telephoned Mr Hunter and explained the situation to him.

He was deeply concerned. 'My dear girl, how awful for you, but I'm so relieved you're not hurt. What about James?'

Gillian hesitated. Mr Hunter didn't know of their separation. 'He's away on business and I don't want to worry him.'

'I see. Now, there's no hurry about returning to the office. Take all the time you need up there in Harbury. I'll phone your neighbour, Sue, and tell her you're staying on for a bit.'

Holly was stretched out on the sofa when Gillian returned to the living-room.

'Was that your employer?' she asked. 'I hope you won't lose your job by being detained.'

Gillian concealed a smile. Holly could hardly care about that since she was here at her insistence.

'It doesn't matter. I'm redundant, anyway, the firm is closing down.'

Later that evening she telephoned the Eidelweiss. It was something she'd been dreading all day. She'd had so little time to think of James over the past few days and she hadn't wanted to think of Barbara Reynolds at all. She experienced a sense of relief when a male voice answered the hotel's phone.

James had not returned, however, and there had been no message from him.

'Did you speak to Barbara Reynolds?' Holly's voice was over-casual as she watched Gillian come into the living-room and sit down.

'No, it was a man,' Gillian paused. 'Who would that be?'

Holly didn't answer for a moment. 'It was probably her brother, Frank,' she said eventually in a low voice.

Roy had said nothing, not even raised his head from the paper he was reading, but Gillian was aware of a tense atmosphere in the room. She remembered his sharp question to Holly about being at the Eidelweiss before the accident and her glib lie in reply. She remembered, too, that well-beaten path from the hotel entrance which led straight to the cottage and nowhere else. But she could only wonder at the atmosphere. As she reminded herself, this family was not her business.

44

By Tuesday evening, her car had still not been repaired, and she knew she could no longer stay at the cottage. For one thing, Holly had completely recovered, although she wouldn't admit it. Gillian was also very perturbed by the way Holly kept clinging to her and she just didn't know how to cope with it. She admitted to herself, she had a sneaking liking for the girl and they might have been friends in different circumstances. But she was at a loss to understand Holly's sudden and ardent attachment to her. After all, the girl knew nothing about her, apart from what she'd overheard at the hotel.

Gillian gripped the edge of the sink with tense, painful fingers as she thought of James. The fact that Barbara was pregnant hurt terribly. Gillian had always longed for a child of her own—the child she'd never had.

She turned away from the sink, swallowing tears. Through blurred eyes she noticed Chris's forgotten plimsoll thrown down by the boiler. Yes, she would have to leave. She was too taken with Chris, too eager to help. Yet how could she help him, or Holly for that matter? She was the one who really needed help.

She had a suspicion, too, that Roy Andrews would be relieved to see her go. Later that night, when the other two had gone to bed, she spoke to him.

'I'm going to Banford tomorrow.'

He didn't raise his head.

'There's been no word of James and I can't impose on you any longer.' She'd rehearsed it so that she would be concise and not say she was sorry to leave Holly and Chris.

'You know best,' he said without expression. 'I'll take you to the station in the morning.'

Going upstairs to pack, she noticed a strip of light under Chris's door. Thinking perhaps he'd fallen asleep with the light on, she gently opened the door. He was sitting in bed, busily poring over a large scrapbook.

'Hey, shouldn't you be asleep?' she whispered.

Instantly, he snapped the book shut and jammed it under the sheet.

'Can't I see it?' she said.

There was a moment's hesitation, then he shook his head violently.

'O K. 'Night, Chris.'

She closed the door quietly and went along to her room. She mustn't wonder about Chris's scrapbook, mustn't wonder about the flash of fear she'd seen in his face. She had to leave and cut herself off from this house.

Roy took her to the station after dropping Chris at school the following morning. Holly had been predictably tearful, but also, Gillian thought, a little scared.

Chris was silent and withdrawn as she said goodbye, and she felt any progress she'd made

46

with him had been lost again.

Roy dumped her bag on the train, said a brief 'goodbye,' and was gone. She would be forgotten very soon by all of them. They had survived without her before Friday night, and they would do so again. Roy Andrews had a tough job with those two, but he was a hard, capable man. He'd obviously learned to cope as best he could. That little Andrews family didn't really need her.

The train gathered speed and she stared out of the window. All this way to see James and it had been of no use. Or had it? She'd found out just how close James and Barbara appeared to be. Perhaps James no longer needed her. She shrugged mentally. No one appeared to need her.

Perhaps it was due to the fact that she was alone for the first time since Friday, that Gillian was able to think clearly. So, if James no longer needed her, why hadn't he told her, why hadn't he honestly contacted her and said he wanted to marry Barbara? Surely she had a right to know. Just as she had a right to know where James was. What if something had happened to her in the accident with Holly? Someone would have contacted James then.

With mounting anger, Gillian realised that Barbara Reynolds must know where James was. How dare they treat her like this! What was she supposed to do? Sit and twiddle her thumbs until they decided to let her know what

47

her future was going to be? Run up and down to Eidelweiss to see if James was ready to speak to her?

Well, she wasn't having that! In fact, she wasn't ever going back to the Eidelweiss at all. Let James come home and see her, she wasn't doing any more running around. He could bring her car with him when he came.

She need never return to Harbury.

CHAPTER THREE

It was a glorious day.

The platforms at Banford station were alive with crowds of people enjoying the first really warm day of the year.

Gillian's journey from Harbury had been punctuated by long delays. She was hot and tired, dishevelled and crumpled.

Taxis were scarce, too, so she had to make her way to the bus station where she had another long wait. Eventually, she arrived at Heather Avenue.

Blossom dipped and swayed overhead as she walked towards the house. In the gardens, children splashed in paddling pools, and fathers half-heartedly struggled with lawnmowers.

Gillian noticed how untidy her garden was. The house too looked sad, with dull, dusty windows. Somehow, she couldn't bear to go in. She passed her gate and turned into Sue Jackson's drive. Here she was sure of a cool drink and some warm company. But there was no reply to her knock.

Feeling dejected she slipped through the gap in the fence to her own house. Opening the front door she found a handful of letters, but they were all circulars, nothing personal.

The rooms seemed to echo emptily, the very tidiness emphasising the absence of people. Suddenly the upheaval of the week-end seemed far away and unreal.

But she didn't want to think about what had happened at Harbury. It would be better to find some hard physical work to exhaust her mind and body.

She went outside again and tackled the garden; first the lawn, then the flower borders.

Two hours later, she locked up the tools, feeling hungry for the first time. She still hadn't spoken to anyone.

Suddenly she remembered that the Eidelweiss Hotel was not aware she'd left Harbury. She dialled the number before she lost her nerve. Barbara Reynolds answered.

She gave her name, aware of the silence at the other end. Her heart seemed to be thumping dreadfully.

'I thought I'd better let you know I've returned to Banford.'

'Thank you,' the girl replied. 'There's ...

there's been no word from Mr Parker.'

Gillian said nothing. She was now fairly certain that Barbara Reynolds must know James's whereabouts, but there was no sense accusing her now, when she was over a hundred miles away.

'I see. Goodnight, then,' she replied formally and hung up.

She allowed herself a somewhat sour smile. The only person she'd spoken to in hours was the woman for whom her husband had left her!

As she tidied away her supper dishes, she thought briefly of the little family she'd left in Harbury. Was Chris secretly looking at his scrapbook again tonight? Was Holly still playing the invalid? She would probably never know...

She'd scarcely switched off the bedside-light when the telephone rang.

James! It had to be him!

No one else knew she was here. He'd returned, or Barbara Reynolds had contacted him. Her mouth went dry. It was four months since she'd spoken to her husband.

With a shaking hand she lifted the receiver.

'Gillian?' The voice was high, familiar. 'It's Sue.'

Her next door neighbour! She didn't know whether she was relieved or disappointed.

'I saw your light when I came home just now. Is everything all right?'

'Fine,' Gillian answered mechanically trying

50

to sound cheerful. 'I got home this afternoon.'

'I'm sorry I was out,' Sue said. 'Would you like to come round now for a nightcap? We could have a chat.'

Gillian knew Sue was concerned, but...

'No ... I won't, thank you. I'm in bed. I did too much gardening when I came home and I'm really tired,' she apologised.

'Well—if you're sure—' Sue seemed reluctant to put down the phone.

'I'll see what I can manage tomorrow,' Gillian promised. Then with a sigh, she added, 'I do need to talk to you—but I've got to go into the office first.'

'Good,' her friend replied, obviously relieved that Gillian wasn't going to bottle up her worries any longer.

'Fine. Sleep well, then,' Sue added and rang off.

Despite the good wishes and her exhaustion, Gillian spent another restless night. She dreamed she was in a crowded ballroom with several hundred people around her, but no one was aware of her.

She woke determined to go out a bit more, and do all the things magazines recommended for lonely people. The thought made her smile. It all seemed so calculated, so unlike her.

As she had expected, her boss, Mr Hunter, fussed over her terribly when she arrived at the office. He made her some watery tea and insisted she sat in the only armchair in the old-fashioned office.

She'd telephoned him and told him about the accident, but he seemed unconvinced that she wasn't walking around with a broken arm or ribs.

'If your car was so badly damaged, you must have been injured,' he said worriedly.

'Just a few bruises and shock.' She tried to sound reassuring, touched that he really cared. 'The best thing for me would be to knuckle down to some work and forget it all as quickly as possible.'

She finished her tea, rose, and rinsed out the cups at the tiny sink in the corner of the office.

'It won't take long to make out the redundancy slips,' Mr Hunter told her. 'I have the money in the safe. The men can be paid off today.'

'Oh!' She turned in surprise. 'I thought they wouldn't finish the contracts until the end of the month?'

Mr Hunter hesitated for a moment, then spread out his hands. He looked half-apologetic, half-pleased.

'I've had an offer for the business, my dear. From someone in the same line. He wants to keep on most of the men.'

'How marvellous,' Gillian said. 'Jobs are difficult to come by these days.'

'True.' He hesitated again. 'I—I said I thought you might be interested in staying on—at least for a while.'

Again she looked at him in surprise. It wasn't like him to make arrangements without consulting her.

'Well—actually, I thought'—he fumbled a little—'you're on your own now, aren't you, my dear?'

Gillian looked out of the window for a moment, then nodded. She felt a comforting hand on her shoulder.

'It didn't work out at the week-end then?' he asked gently. 'I'm sorry, I shouldn't interfere, but I've noticed you haven't been yourself lately. I presumed you and James were—'

'He left, about four months ago,' she said bluntly, trying to avoid the shocked look in the older man's eyes.

'I went to Harbury to see him at the week-end. He wasn't there. I'm—I'm still trying to make contact.'

Suddenly, she made up her mind and turned positively to him.

'Yes, I shall need a job.'

It didn't take her long to tie up all the loose ends of Hunter Heating. The books had always been kept in impeccable order and she made out a very detailed catalogue of work to be completed and accounts due. By lunchtime everything was in order and the men had their money.

After collecting some sandwiches and a carton of milk from the shop round the corner she sat quietly in the shabby office and enjoyed

53

her lunch. The peace and familiarity of these surroundings would be a comfort to her through whatever lay ahead. Yes, she was glad she could go on working here.

It was almost three o'clock when Mr Hunter returned with his successor.

Tall and broad shouldered, Paul Osgood was a good twenty years younger than Mr Hunter. He was expensively dressed in a cream, pinstriped suit with matching silk shirt that set off his deep tan to advantage. He had an expensive smile which contrasted dramatically with small, narrow eyes.

'So you're the treasure.' He held out a confident hand to Gillian.

'How do you do, Mr Osgood,' she murmured, formally shaking hands.

'I need someone to take good care of me.' He grinned at her. 'From Harry's description you're just the girl for me.'

'I hope I'll be able to help you over the first few hurdles,' Gillian said primly.

'Oh, I'm not anticipating any problems. The changeover to my way of working will be smooth as silk.'

Gillian wondered briefly if she had made the right decision. Then she realised she hadn't decided to stay on—Paul Osgood had just assumed that she would!

She glanced at Mr Hunter. He looked bewildered and uneasy. He had built his business on trust, good manners, and reliable

54

workmanship, and had never seen any need to change.

Gillian was inclined to agree with him, but she knew she must allow Mr Osgood a chance. Perhaps his changes would be constructive.

'See you in the morning.' He winked at her and strode out of the office, Mr Hunter following forlornly behind.

* * *

It was almost four o'clock before Gillian went round to Sue's. Over coffee and a ridiculously large slice of cream cake, she briefly sketched the week-end she'd spent in Harbury.

'I should have told you before about James leaving home, but ... Oh, I suppose it was pride that held me back—and hope that he'd return before anyone really noticed.' She smiled briefly. 'But there's no point in hiding it any longer. He isn't coming back.'

'You may be wrong there,' Sue said quietly. 'James has always been a fair person. If he'd made up his mind he'd have let you know.'

Gillian weighed that up for a few moments.

'No, I think James will stay with Barbara Reynolds,' she said finally. 'After all, there is the child coming.' She had no idea of the depth of longing in her voice.

Sue passed over a plate of biscuits.

'This boy—Chris. He's had a rough time, hasn't he?'

'Oh, Sue, if you could have seen him. He's locked in a world of silence, not even talking to his dog. If only someone could get through to him.'

'You seem to have made contact.'

Gillian shrugged and said nothing.

'He could have been a substitute, you know, Gillian.' Sue didn't look at her friend.

'A substitute?' Gillian lowered her cup and stared at Sue. 'You mean—a child for me to mother?' she whispered.

'That might be putting it a bit strongly.' Sue looked concerned.

'A substitute was the last thing I was looking for!' Gillian spoke sharply. 'I was too upset by what had happened.'

She took a biscuit absentmindedly.

'I think Chris and I hit it off because I was a total stranger, and didn't know anything about his mother's death. He was just a little more relaxed, that's all.' She paused for a moment.

'Anyway, it's all behind me now. I just hope someone gets through to Chris—and soon.'

'For his sake I hope so, too,' Sue said. 'You're going to carry on at Hunter Heating?' She changed the subject briskly.

'It looks like it.'

'You don't sound too enthusiastic.'

Gillian laughed.

'I'm not. Paul Osgood seems a bit flashy to me, but then maybe I'm old-fashioned like Mr Hunter.'

'But you need the job?' Sue asked quietly.

'Desperately.' Gillian sighed.

'So you're keeping on the house?'

'I can't sell it until I know what James has decided.'

'It is a lot to keep paying for the upkeep when ... when ...' Sue faltered.

Gillian sighed again. 'I have no choice, have I?'

* * *

The first thing that met her eyes when she opened the office door next morning was a large bowl of roses sitting on her desk.

'Oh, how lovely,' she said involuntarily.

'Thought you'd like them.' Paul Osgood rose from the arm of the chair beaming with self-satisfaction.

'And it's only a start. I'm going to transform this office. Out goes the Ark, in comes the twentieth century.'

'Oh, it isn't as bad as that!' Gillian protested, trying not to sound annoyed.

'Be honest, Gillian! You can't enjoy working in this mausoleum?'

Gillian deliberately moved the bowl of flowers to a side table.

'I enjoyed working here with Mr Hunter,' she said quietly. 'That's the only reason I stayed on.'

'Loyalty is above price.' His answer was so

57

smooth she wondered if he had really taken her point.

He disappeared for an hour or two while she made out circular letters to all their customers telling them about the changeover from Hunter Heating to Osgood. She had queried the firm's new solitary name.

'Of course, I'll continue to install central heating, but I just want the name Osgood, and nothing more. I aim to branch out in as many directions as many customers may want. Eventually the people of this town are going to say, "Let's go to Osgood" when they want something—anything! It's a new image, Gillian.'

When she made him some coffee midmorning, he returned to his favourite theme again.

'As I said—the new image. It begins here, right in this office. Out goes the antique setting—in comes chrome and glass.'

Next day, the decor consultants arrived. Paul Osgood was anxious that she should have a say in the choice of carpet and wallpaper, but she thought it was more tactful to decline. She sensed her taste would in no way please Paul Osgood.

It seemed, however, that money was no object. He ordered nothing but the best carpets, wallpaper, and furniture.

When the first of the salesmen who had supplied Hunter Heating with materials arrived on his regular visit, Gillian greeted him, as usual, with a cup of coffee. But Paul Osgood was not so welcoming.

'Sorry, Osgood will not be placing orders with your firm,' he told the young man.

'Why?' The salesman was genuinely perplexed. His firm had been supplying Hunter Heating for years.

'You're too expensive,' Paul Osgood told him. 'I can get better materials elsewhere.'

'Not better, Mr Osgood—cheaper.'

Paul Osgood opened the door. 'Good afternoon,' he said smoothly.

He then gave Gillian an order to place with new suppliers.

She looked at the name on the paper.

'Mr Hunter would never deal with this company,' she began hesitantly. 'Their materials are shoddy and unreliable. The men don't like fitting them.'

'Too bad. They can look for other jobs if this one doesn't suit, can't they?

'Please do as I say, Gillian. This is Osgood now, not Hunter Heating any longer. The age of the fuddy-duddy is over.'

Gillian jumped up. 'That was uncalled for!'

'The truth often is,' he retorted as he left the office.

Next day Gillian was determined to try to cope with everything as calmly as possible and not let Paul Osgood's derisory remarks get under her skin. The estimate for the new office

59

furnishings arrived and she showed it to him, wondering how on earth he could afford the prices. She didn't wonder for long.

'Wow! Still we'll make it. Now you see why I got rid of that expensive supplier!

'Now—let's take a look at the accounts due. Pass me the ledger, please, Gillian. We'll nail the bad debtors.'

Thoughtfully, she opened the desk drawer and took out the accounts book.

'I wouldn't call these people debtors, Mr Osgood. We have always given our customers at least a month to pay.'

'Bad policy. Send out final accounts at once. Payment by return.'

'You can't do that—'

'There's nothing I can't do, Gillian.' Again the smoothness ruffled Gillian.

'You don't understand. Some of these people have been customers of ours for years.' Gillian indicated the list.

'And they've been taking advantage of doddery old Hunter for all that time.'

'Mr Hunter is not doddery!' Gillian flashed, unable to hide her feelings any longer.

'Oh, be your age, Gillian. He and his attitude to business went out with feather boas. Now, get these accounts sent out today. Type "overdue" on the envelope—in red. That'll make them pay up.'

She was appalled. 'You're embarrassing the customers.'

60

'So what? I want the money. That's the way to get it.'

Gillian stood up.

'Then get it yourself, Mr Osgood. I certainly won't do it for you!'

She picked up her bag and made for the door.

'Suit yourself,' he said. 'You're easily replaced!'

Gillian was still shaking when she got home. She'd burned her boats now, all right. She knew enough of Paul Osgood to realise he'd never take her back—she knew she wouldn't go, anyway.

* * *

'Home early, aren't you, Gillian?' Sue called across the fence. 'Some people get marvellous jobs these days.'

'I walked out.'

Her friend's eyes were round with surprise. 'Just like that?'

'Oh, I couldn't stand him,' Gillian said. 'Come in and have coffee and I'll tell you all about it.'

She picked up a couple of letters from the mat and led the way into the kitchen. As she made the coffee she told Sue what had happened.

'I don't like the sound of him myself,' Sue said. 'But just to walk out, it's so out of

61

character for you, Gillian.'

'I've changed.' There was an unaccustomed hardness in her voice. 'A lot of things have happened to me recently to make me see life differently.

'Anyway, it's done. I could never work with someone like that.'

She picked up the envelopes and slit them open. One contained her bank statement. She studied it ruefully.

'It's all very well making the grand gesture, but now I'm the proud destitute! I hope I don't run out of tights soon.'

She unfolded the letter from the second envelope. 'Oh, no!'

'What is it? Word from James?' Sue asked quickly.

'No—nothing like that. A bill for roof repairs. I'd clean forgotten all about it.' She passed the bill across to her friend.

'Seventy pounds? How could you forget that?'

'I didn't know it was going to amount to that! And goodness knows what my car will cost to repair. What am I going to do?'

'Ask James,' Sue said crisply.

'No! I'm determined not to pester him—even if I knew where he was,' she finished a little bitterly.

She lifted her bank statement again.

'When I pay the bill, I'm cleaned out ... and no salary coming in.'

'You could go back to Paul Osgood and eat humble pie,' Sue suggested.

'I'll never eat humble pie, or crawl to Paul Osgood—or anyone else again!

'Over the last few months, I've been more or less ignored by James. Then last week-end I was criticised by Barbara Reynolds for not getting in touch with him. On top of that, I was blamed by Roy Andrews for knocking his sister down when she ran out in front of me!

'I feel a little bit like a coconut shy—set me up and knock me down. Or rather I felt like a coconut shy—but not any longer.'

*   *   *

For the next week, Gillian trudged round employment agencies looking for work. Anything that was remotely suitable seemed to be miles away—and she had no car. She managed to get a day's work here and there, but by the end of the next week she was exhausted.

One evening, she called round to see Mr Hunter to explain why she'd walked out on Paul Osgood.

Mr Hunter was very understanding.

'You couldn't do anything else, my dear. I can't see his business succeeding with the attitudes he's adopting. You've no idea of the number of phone calls I've had from customers complaining about his demanding letters.'

Gillian nodded, concealing a smile. They would always be 'our customers' to Mr Hunter.

Grace, his wife, had made a delicious supper, and Gillian found she was relaxing for the first time in a few weeks. They fussed over her almost as if she was their daughter.

'Grace and I are off to Eastbourne next week, Gillian,' Mr Hunter told her. 'A longish holiday. We'll just stay until we feel homesick.'

'That's marvellous. You need a really good holiday,' she told them. 'I'm sure this changeover of the business has been quite a strain on both of you.'

'On you, too, my dear,' Mrs Hunter said with a shy smile.

'That's why we'd like you to come with us,' Mr Hunter said quickly.

'You could do with a break—luxury hotel, relaxing atmosphere. And you've plenty of time to find a job when we come back. Please—it will give us great pleasure. It's our treat to you, a thank you for being such a loyal secretary and friend over the years.'

For a few moments, Gillian was unable to speak. It was such a touching gesture and so kind of them to think of her. At the thought of the holiday all her worries seemed to diminish a little.

'Thank you very much,' she said slowly. 'You're both so kind, but—'

She paused. Her worries wouldn't go away;

64

she'd have to stay and deal with them.

'I can't accept,' she finished at last. 'There's James, and the house, and I really need a permanent job.'

The elderly couple looked quite crestfallen.

'Perhaps we could help,' Mr Hunter offered uncertainly.

But Gillian refused firmly. She was only able to finally leave by promising to try to visit Eastbourne one week-end.

She arrived home, tired and almost at the end of her tether.

Going into the living-room, she kicked off her shoes and lay back on the chair. There was no use going to bed too soon. She was over-tired and probably overfed; she'd never sleep.

The ring of the telephone startled her. As usual, her heart began to race as she hurriedly picked up the receiver.

'Hello,' she said.

'Roy Andrews here—How are you?' The voice sounded deeper than she remembered.

Surprised, Gillian sat down. She'd never expected to hear from him again.

'Fine. I'm fine. How is everything with you?'

'Holly—is coming on.'

'I'm glad to hear that,' Gillian murmured, wondering what on earth he wanted to speak to her about.

'She wants to see you again,' he said baldly.

'Oh ... I see.' Gillian was still puzzled. 'Perhaps I could call and see her when I come to fetch my car. Though goodness knows when it will be ready—they're having trouble getting parts.'

'Chris is missing you too.'

'Really?' How did Roy know? Had Chris spoken?

'How ... how did—'

'He keeps putting flowers in the room you used when you were here.'

She was unable to detect any expression in his voice at all.

'Oh. When I come to collect my car, I'll call—'

'I'm phoning to ask if you would come back here for a while,' he interrupted swiftly.

'You mean to stay? I'm afraid I couldn't!'

'Why? Have you found another job?'

'No, not yet—'

'Your husband hasn't come back, has he?'

'No, but—'

'Then you could come. There's nothing to keep you in Banford just now, is there?'

'Look, hang on a moment,' she said a little crossly. 'You're not giving me time to think.'

'I'm sorry,' he said quickly. 'It's just that Holly's been pestering me to phone you—'

He still doesn't mince his words, Gillian thought.

'She's really not herself again. And I know Chris would like you to come back, too. I certainly could use someone to look after them both.'

She smiled ruefully. The invitation was not exactly gift-wrapped!

'Look,' he continued. 'You think it over. I'll phone tomorrow night for your answer.'

Slowly, Gillian put down the receiver. Really, the man was being a bit presumptuous. Didn't he think she had enough problems without becoming involved in his?

She went to bed too weary to think straight.

* * *

Next day at the agency she found she had only one more day's work. There were no permanent jobs available for secretaries. At the end of the week she'd have enough money to pay the bills—but little else.

She was also beginning to despair that James would ever contact her. Would she have to confront him? That meant going to Harbury again.

Of course, if James knew she was waiting there for him it might hasten his return—force his hand as it were. Their affairs had to come to some conclusion not only for her peace of mind but for more mundane financial problems.

For the same financial reasons, she couldn't afford to wait for him at The Eidelweiss, or any other hotel for that matter.

Perhaps Roy Andrews' was a good idea after all. She could shut up the house and save expenses, she could collect her car when it was ready and, just as important, it would give her something to do to keep her mind occupied. After all, it was only a week or so.

She sighed. She wasn't at all keen to go back to the cottage, but it did seem a sensible solution in her present circumstances.

When Roy Andrews phoned that evening she told him she'd come. He seemed relieved.

'I'll meet you off the afternoon train tomorrow,' he said.

It would be a rush, but Gillian was glad. Now that she'd made up her mind, as she told Sue the next morning before she left, she couldn't wait to get away.

This time the journey to Harbury wasn't nearly so long and she began to look forward to seeing Holly and Chris again. It would be good to be in a house with people to talk to. She realised now, how lonely she'd been all those months since James had gone.

She jumped down from the train immediately it stopped. Roy Andrews was there, unsmiling.

He picked up her suitcase and nodded to her.

'You understand that this is Holly's idea.'

He was as blunt as usual. 'As far as I'm concerned, this is purely a business arrangement.'

'A business arrangement?'

'Yes. You've come here as a house-keeper. I'll pay you a wage. I wouldn't ask you to work for nothing. I need your help, but not your charity.'

CHAPTER FOUR

Despite Roy's rather offhand welcome and his perfunctory attempts at conversation during the journey, Gillian had a feeling of pleasant anticipation as they approached the cottage.

Holly and Chris had obviously been watching for the car; the front door was flung open as soon as they drew up.

Holly, impetuous as ever, rushed out and gave Gillian a welcoming hug. Over her shoulder, Gillian saw Chris waiting by the door, a little uncertain, but with a faint gleam of welcome in his eyes.

'It's good to see you again, Holly,' Gillian said warmly.

She walked towards Chris and held out her hand.

'Hi, Chris.'

He hesitated only for a moment then took her hand and shook it with childish enthusiasm.

'How's your dog?' she asked. 'Still chasing sticks?'

He nodded, and she realised she had asked him a question that could be answered by a gesture. So, he was still unable or unwilling to talk.

69

'Chris, will you help with Gillian's bag?' his father called.

The boy darted past her and eagerly collected her bag from the car.

'I'll make you some tea, Gillian,' Holly said. 'Was the journey dreadful?'

'Not really,' Gillian said absentmindedly, since she'd noticed Chris lingering at the foot of the stairs with her bag. 'I think I'll just slip upstairs and change, though.'

She followed the boy up to the bedroom she'd used the last time she was here. Chris had put her bag down by the wardrobe and was standing by the window trying to look nonchalant. She saw the tight, almost squashed, bunch of flowers jammed into a cracked flower vase.

'Spring flowers—how lovely.' She turned to Chris. 'Are they for me?' He nodded and she lightly fingered the sprays of forsythia, flowering currant, and the straggly bluebells which dwarfed the tiny primroses.

'Did you pick these near the cottage?'

He pointed to the primroses and the forsythia outside in the garden.

'And the others—did you find them in the woods?'

It was only a guess. All she knew of the surrounding area was a wood between the cottage and The Eidelweiss Hotel. He went to the window, throwing his arm wide as if to indicate that the bluebells were scattered

70

fairly far.

'I'd like to go there if I may. I've always loved bluebells. It's such a pity they don't bloom all the year round. They make everyone so happy,' she said.

Chris looked at her for a moment, then transferred his gaze to the bluebells. She wondered if she'd said anything that had touched a memory—of his mother, perhaps?

She really must ask Holly some details. It wouldn't be prying, but she simply had to know, if only to avoid further hurt to Chris.

Downstairs, Holly had made tea, and she carried the tray into the comfortable living-room. Holly chattered to her about inconsequential matters and Chris passed the biscuits. Gillian was amused, yet pleased, to see that Chris ate steadily and remorselessly until the plate was empty. In every other respect he was a normal boy. It only needed something to unlock his tongue.

As she sipped her tea, Gillian realised that Holly and Chris would treat her as one of the family. Roy, she was sure, wouldn't.

She was quite glad, in a strange way. She had a job to do here and she wanted to earn her wages honestly. How long it would last was an unanswered question, and what she would do beyond that she had no idea. The future could only be resolved when James and she met again.

Until then, she had to live each day as it

71

came. She knew she would get along well with Holly and Chris, but she must be careful not to become so involved that they would depend on her—or she on them, for that matter.

As soon as tea was finished, though, she found herself launched into work.

'There are some chops and vegetables in the pantry,' Holly told her. 'I've left tonight's meal for you to cope with.'

She grinned disarmingly. 'I remember your cooking when you were here last. I'm strictly beans-on-toast standard.'

Gillian picked up the tea-tray and made for the door. 'Just show me where to find things, Holly.'

The girl followed her into the kitchen.

'You won't find much here,' she said. 'I'm afraid I wasn't any more organised than Carol. Anyway, Chris has been having his main meal at school and Roy has a good lunch at work, I think.'

'And you, Holly? What's your job?' Gillian was curious.

'Oh, arts and crafts,' she said vaguely, drifting away towards the door. 'Sometimes, in the winter, I teach at an evening class run by the local arts centre. Do you mind if I run a bath now?'

Hardly waiting for an answer, she slipped out of the kitchen.

Gillian took a long, assessing look at the kitchen. She had never liked working in someone else's domain. Every woman put her own imprint on her kitchen and she supposed Roy's wife had been no exception, but there was no trace of her now. There seemed to be little organisation and Gillian could see she had a big task in front of her. Chris had gone out into the garden and there was no reason why she could not start now.

On her last visit, she'd noticed a dining-room, which was obviously rarely used.

Impulsively, she set off on a tour of inspection. She was standing looking at a beautiful rosewood dining-table thinking how badly it needed care, when Roy entered the room.

'Finding everything all right?' He looked surprised.

'Oh, yes, just taking stock of what we need, including cleaning materials. I'll have a fairly long shopping list,' she said half-apologetically.

He shrugged. 'I thought that would be the case. We've just been ticking over for the last year.'

He waved his arm round the room. 'Nothing has really been tackled on a big scale—like spring cleaning.'

'Oh, well, that's a yearly job anyway.'

'Goodness knows when it was last done. Several years ago by the look of it.'

She looked at him in surprise. What had his wife done with her time?

73

'I was abroad for some time,' he said shortly, then turned and left the room.

Gillian watched the door close behind him. Now she knew the reason for his tanned skin and bleached hair, so noticeable when they'd first met by her wrecked car. But why had he been abroad and Chris and his wife here?

* * *

It was evident that the family enjoyed the evening meal and Roy insisted afterwards that everyone help clear up.

'I can cope,' Gillian said.

'I know, but we don't intend to make a slave out of you,' he replied.

Gillian conceded, glad to know he was fair-minded.

'Actually, I have a job I hope Chris will help me with.' She turned to look at the boy. 'I noticed most of the plants in the house need re-potting. We might also be able to take some cuttings. Can you help me, Chris?'

He nodded eagerly and ran out of the kitchen. Before they had finished clearing away the dishes, Chris had the kitchen table covered with the pot plants. She had no idea whether the task would appeal to him or not, but she guessed he was bored and might like plants.

'I think there's a bag of potting compost in the garden shed,' Roy said, looking at the array of straggly plants. 'Would that be of any use?'

74

'Yes, please,' Gillian said.

'Chris?'

Before the name was out of Roy's mouth, Chris had flung open the back door and was racing across the garden.

'It seems you have a willing apprentice,' Roy said with a wry smile and left the kitchen.

On his return, she showed Chris how to take cuttings.

'Now we'll put them in a glass of water for about a week to allow them to root. After that we can pot them.'

She was surprised that he was so adept at everything. The small fingers were gentle and skilful with the fragile cuttings.

'Have you done this before?' she asked him, but he shook his head vigorously.

By bedtime, she was exhausted. It hadn't even been a full day's work at the cottage and she wondered if she would be able to cope. As she wearily undressed, however, she realised her tiredness was as much due to strain as work.

As she drew back the covers of the bed, something fluttered inside. She started and jumped back, thinking it was a dreaded creepie crawlie of some kind. But nothing moved and she cautiously approached the bed again and drew the sheet back. It was a piece of paper—a drawing. Gently, she lifted it up. It was a drawing of a bluebell, but a drawing of such delicacy and beauty that it caught her breath. Chris certainly had talent.

* * *

Next day being Sunday, Roy said he didn't want the house turned upside down that day, so she contented herself with making the meals and tidying the bedrooms. Here, Chris helped, too, and shyly showed her round his room.

Gillian could see that Roy had spared no effort in providing his son with an interesting and imaginative room. There were books of every description, from encyclopedia to picture annuals and adventure stories.

Model aircraft swung on thin wire from the ceiling, games and toys were in plentiful supply, and the furniture was sturdy, yet comfortable. But there were no drawings or paintings, as she might have expected in a room which housed such an artistic child.

The afternoon was fine and Gillian suggested a walk, so that she might familiarise herself with the surroundings. To her surprise, Roy and Holly came, too. As she had hoped, they came upon the bluebell woods.

'What a sea of bluebells.' Gillian spread her arms wide. 'Aren't they magnificent?'

'I believe Chris put some in your room,' Roy said.

'Yes, such a lovely bunch and one rather special one.' She turned to look at Chris and was amazed to see a brief look of panic in his eyes.

'Which one was that?' Roy asked.

'Oh, a drawing—it's very good.'

Gillian was hesitant in the face of Chris's distress. Perhaps she'd said the wrong thing. Perhaps he should have drawn one for Roy. She was aware of Roy's surprise.

'Draw one for your father, Chris,' she said quickly. 'Here, I have some paper and a pencil in my bag.'

With quick, nervous movements, the boy took the paper and pencil and began to draw. Then, unsmilingly, he handed the drawing over to Roy.

Glancing over his shoulder, Gillian saw a rough, crude drawing, one that a child of Chris's years might very well do if he had no interest in art, or flowers, or conveying a message.

Roy looked for a moment at the drawing, then smiled. 'That's nice, son. May I keep it?' He looked at Chris.

The boy, anxiety gone from his face, smiled slightly in return and nodded.

Gillian tried to hide her dismay. Why had she received the beautiful drawing and Roy the crude one? True, Chris drew today's bluebell very hurriedly, but the crudeness of the drawing was very evident. Deliberate. The only conclusion was that there was some kind of barrier between them—one that Chris had set up.

77

It wasn't surprising that Roy was having such difficulty in communicating. He was probably quite unaware of that barrier. Just as he was unaware that Chris could draw beautifully. There had been no disappointment in Roy's voice, no expectation of something better. He obviously had no idea of his son's talent.

She found her thoughts suddenly arrested when they came upon a path that seemed familiar to her. With a start, she realised this was the shortcut from Roy's cottage to the Eidelweiss Hotel.

She felt a nervous twinge, realising she would have to take this path tomorrow. Tomorrow, she had to face Barbara Reynolds again.

She wasn't looking forward to the encounter, but another telephone call would be a waste of time. A personal visit, coupled with the fact that she was staying in the area, would surely force Barbara and James to face up to the situation.

Later that evening, Gillian looked in on Chris to say good night. She took her drawing with her.

'Why, Chris ... why this one for me and the other for your father?'

He only shook his head.

'Don't you think he'd be hurt if he saw this?' she asked.

In answer, he snatched the beautiful drawing

78

from her hand and tore it into shreds.

She sat for a moment at the foot of his bed, saddened by his action.

'I wasn't going to show it to him,' she said quietly, trying to sound calm. 'I just meant, that if your father knew you could draw so well, he'd be so proud of you.'

He was still shaking his head violently, but it was the tears in his eyes that shocked her into silence.

She hesitated for only a second. Whatever was at the root of his problem, and whether it was her business or not, the child needed comforting. She drew him close to her.

'I won't tell him, Chris, I promise—until you say.' She left it open like that. His father would have to know one day, when Chris was ready.

*   *   *

Next morning, she was up by seven o'clock to make breakfast for Roy and Chris.

'If you come with us in the morning, you can drop me at the office and keep the car for shopping,' Roy had told her on the Sunday evening.

After breakfast, they set off, dropping Chris at the local primary school. It was a bright, cheerful building, not too large. It had an air of friendliness about its open play area. Chris left the car without a fuss and waved a casual good-bye.

79

'Chris seems to like his school,' she commented.

'Yes.' Roy drew away from the kerb, watching the traffic and the children crossing. 'After the accident, it was suggested I send him to a special school, but I didn't want that.'

'A change in schools could have deepened the disturbance,' Gillian said thoughtfully.

Roy turned quickly to look at her in surprise.

'Yes, that's exactly what I thought. But it's more than a year now and still—no sign.'

'Was he a quiet boy before?'

There was a long silence. 'I worked abroad for two years. Sometimes I had to get to know Chris all over again on my leaves.'

Gillian said nothing. She was beginning to understand quite a few things now. Little things, like Roy not knowing when the house had last been spring-cleaned, and big things, like being unaware of his son's talent. It looked as if the gulf between Roy and his son had been there before the accident.

'Will you collect Chris from school this afternoon?' he said, as he drew up at an anonymous office block.

'Yes, of course. Shall I call here for you at—'

'No thanks. I'll get a lift from a colleague or, better still, walk.'

'Walk!'

He laughed briefly. 'I'm a design engineer, but trained to work abroad on big projects for

80

the developing world. I love open spaces and wide panorama.'

He turned and saw her questioning look. 'I came back, for Chris's sake,' he said simply, then shrugged. 'Unfortunately, I'm not a desk man, I long for the open air, so—'

'So you'll walk,' she finished.

He nodded and slid out of the driving seat. 'The car's all yours,' he finished, and strode into the office block.

The shopping took Gillian longer than she'd anticipated, mainly because she was unfamiliar with the shops and the layout of Harbury, and it was late in the morning before she returned to the cottage. Holly, looking fragile and rather beautiful in cream slacks and sweater, came out to greet her.

'I won't be long getting lunch. I know you want to be in town by one-thirty.'

Holly, however, wasn't so enthusiastic. 'I'm in no hurry. Tomorrow would do.'

'I thought Roy said—' Gillian began.

'I know what Roy said,' Holly interrupted abruptly, 'but this is my life, not his.

'I know he wants me to start work again at the craft boutique, but I just can't turn on creativity you know, Gillian. Artistic people have to be inspired, they need to have no other problems. I'm still not quite myself after the car accident.'

Gillian hid a smile. Holly was really just like a petulant child. She certainly knew how to get

81

her own way, but she remembered Roy's request.

'If Holly seems reluctant to go to the boutique, take her there in the car. Don't take no for an answer. She won't listen to me. Perhaps, she will to you. She needs to build her life again and she needs a good hearty push to get her going.'

Gillian eventually had her way and took Holly to the boutique, at the right time. Turning the car, she drove straight back to the cottage and parked it there. Then she made her way to the path through the woods to the Eidelweiss Hotel.

She felt a little guilty at forcing Holly to go into town, but she had to be alone this afternoon. She must see Barbara Reynolds. Roy and Holly were aware of the situation existing between her and James, but she didn't want them to become involved in her problems.

The path came out at the back of the Eidelweiss Hotel and Gillian noticed two small chalet bungalows, evidently used by the hotel staff as private accommodation. It occurred to her that anyone could go from here to Roy's cottage without being seen by the hotel staff.

She, however, went boldly round to the front of the hotel and walked straight in. The foyer was empty.

She walked towards the reception desk, past the display cabinets containing the antique jewellery and silhouettes which she remembered from her last visit. As she had expected, Barbara Reynolds was behind the reception desk. Her eyes flared in surprise at the sight of Gillian.

Outwardly calm, but inwardly taut and nervous, Gillian spoke.

'I'm back,' she said, 'staying at the Andrews' cottage.'

It wasn't what she'd meant to say and she tried to remember her carefully rehearsed, precise, no-nonsense speech. But before she could begin again, a slim dark figure slid behind the desk to stand beside Barbara.

'Staying with the Andrews? You must be a friend of Holly's,' the man said quickly. 'How nice to meet you. I'm Frank Reynolds, Barbara's brother.'

Gillian had no option but to take his proffered hand, and he shook it warmly.

'I know we haven't met before, or I would certainly have remembered,' he said smoothly.

In fact, thought Gillian, everything about him was smooth.

He was of average height, stockily built, with a smooth complexion, almost olive in tone. His hair, eyebrows, and eyes were all dark. His suit was cleverly cut, but not of particularly good quality. The whole impression was one of suavity. A real smooth operator, Gillian found herself thinking irrationally.

'Are you going to tell me your name or do I

have to guess?' he said teasingly.

'Oh—Gillian Parker,' she supplied, a little embarrassed.

She was aware of Barbara tensing as she spoke.

'Mrs Gillian Parker?' Now his voice was definitely amused. 'How intriguing.'

'Mrs Parker has come to see me,' Barbara said tightly.

'How very civilised. Perhaps, of course, since we haven't met before, you are a friend of Mr Andrews?' he asked.

For some reason, Gillian felt her answer was of vital importance to Frank Reynolds.

'I knew Holly first,' she said carelessly, giving nothing away. 'Are you a friend of Mr Andrews?' she asked boldly.

'No,' was his curt reply. 'But I was a good friend of his wife's. A very good friend, actually.'

'Will you please come into the office, Mrs Parker?' Barbara Reynolds interrupted edgily. 'Look after Reception, Frank.'

'We'll meet again, Mrs Parker. I'll see to that,' was his farewell.

Not if I can help it, Gillian said grimly to herself, following Barbara Reynolds to the hotel's office.

'Do sit down.'

Barbara walked quickly to a desk and sat down behind it, as if trying to hide the fact of her pregnancy. She was wearing the same outfit

84

as on the day Gillian had met her before, a flowery smock top, with the heavy antique bird brooch fastened in the tie.

'Now, how can—' she began when the telephone interrupted her. 'Excuse me.'

The telephone call gave Gillian an opportunity to compose herself and she was able to look round. The hotel's office was well furnished, with a good thick carpet and comfortable chairs. There were two photographs on the wall, obviously of the hotel before and after extensions, and one rather good oil painting. It was a rugged mountain scene and the artist had captured the harshness of the view.

Barbara Reynolds put down the telephone and began talking at once.

'I apologise for my brother. He's a little impetuous.'

Gillian inclined her head in acknowledgement. 'Is he part of the hotel staff?'

'No, he has his own business. "Skua antiques." You may have seen the display cabinets in the hall.' She absently fingered the silver brooch.

Gillian stood up. 'I shan't waste any more of your time. Please tell James I'm staying at the Andrews' cottage. He can contact me there when he returns.'

To her credit, Barbara didn't pretend this

85

time that she was ignorant of James's whereabouts.

'I understand.'

* * *

Gillian left immediately and hurried back through the woodland path to Roy's cottage. She had gone to the hotel, nervous about speaking to Barbara, but her thoughts on the return walk were more occupied with Frank Reynolds. She didn't like him at all, and she couldn't forget the insinuation in his voice when he spoke of Roy's wife and himself.

Half an hour later, she was in the car outside Chris's school. He came out and she noted the quick smile of pleasure on his face when he saw her waiting in the car. She chattered inconsequentially on the way home, and was aware that he nodded and smiled in the seat behind her.

As she began to prepare the meal, he busied himself laying the table and generally being useful to her. She didn't fuss over him, just treated him as naturally as possible.

The days began to fall into the same pattern. She'd take Chris and Roy in the morning. Roy was happy for her to have the car, to drop Holly at the boutique in the afternoon and collect Chris again later.

While they were all out, she was able to come to grips with the cleaning and slowly the house began to look more cared for, to gleam and shine, to exude a warmth. Everyone seemed to be a little more relaxed. Chris was everywhere, helping and hindering. One day, Gillian noticed Roy watching Chris with thoughtful eyes.

Chris gave him a quick smile and returned the plant pot he was examining to the window ledge. Outside, his dog barked and he turned quickly to Roy.

'O.K, off you go. I'll help Gillian finish the dishes.'

He rose from his chair and came over to the draining board. Watching the smiles they exchanged, Gillian realised, there obviously wasn't a total barrier between Chris and his father.

In the silence between her and Roy, there was a sudden sound. A long, clear whistle. It came from outside, from the garden.

As if in reply, the dog barked. Together, they turned and looked out of the window. Thumper was running towards Chris.

Roy turned to look at Gillian. 'That was Chris,' he whispered excitedly. 'That was Chris—whistling!'

She nodded, smiling.

Roy threw down the tea towel and sat down at the table again. His hands were trembling.

'That's the first time—there's been anything,' he said shakily, then looked up. 'Just a small thing, but ... I can't help feeling you're behind this, Gillian.'

87

She shook her head. 'I haven't done anything. Perhaps everyone is more relaxed, now that things are more organised in the house.'

'It's more than that,' he replied. 'I don't understand though. You've no children of your own, yet you are good with Chris.'

'I used to be a children's nurse.' She shrugged. 'In hospital, they need more than just medical care. I suppose that experience is helping now.

'It's nothing to do with me personally.' She paused then added quietly, 'You were the one he wanted to please.'

Roy said nothing, just looked out of the window. As he watched his son's running figure, she could see the hope and happiness in his eyes.

Holly burst into the kitchen then. 'Isn't it a lovely evening? How about a walk, Gillian?'

'Not at the moment. There's really quite a few things I'd like to do.'

'You could help, Holly, you know.' Roy's tone was only slightly admonishing, not so critical of Holly as usual.

'I've been busy. I've begun working on some bits and pieces for the boutique,' she said hurriedly.

'On the telephone?' Roy asked lazily. 'You've been speaking to someone for half an hour.'

'Business contacts.' She shrugged, then

turned to Gillian. 'What about that walk?'

'Yes, all right. Perhaps Chris would like to come, too?'

'No!' Holly stopped abruptly.

'I mean, it might be tiring for him. We could be late in coming back.'

Gillian looked at her in surprise, but then Roy spoke quietly.

'I expect you could do with some fresh air, Gillian. I'll see to Chris tonight.'

Although Gillian was not really anxious to go with Holly, she realised if she was out of the way it might be an opportunity for Roy and Chris to continue that contact that had been made earlier.

'Fine, I'll just finish—' She turned to Holly, who was covertly consulting her watch.

'Oh, leave it till we come home. Come on, I've got your jacket.'

Although it was obvious Holly was anxious to be off, Gillian insisted on speaking to Chris in the garden and telling him she'd be in to say good night when she came home.

They set off along the path towards the Eidelweiss, then Holly suddenly turned off between two trees. Gillian was just able to discern a faint path here, one she hadn't noticed the other day. Holly strode ahead.

'Not so fast.' Gillian laughed. 'I thought this was to be a quiet stroll.'

* * *

Suddenly, Holly stopped dead in front of her. Gillian could just see a small clearing beyond her and the outline of someone standing there.

'Ah, at last,' a voice said.

Holly nimbly stepped aside and Gillian saw the person was Frank Reynolds.

'Why, Frank, I didn't know you liked walking.' Even to Gillian's ears, Holly's voice sounded strained.

'Didn't you,' he answered smoothly. 'Good evening, Mrs Parker.'

Holly's head whipped round. 'Do you know each other?' she asked Gillian, her voice still tense.

'I met Miss Reynolds' brother when I visited her at the hotel a few days ago,' Gillian answered coolly.

'Oh, I see.' Holly relaxed noticeably. 'I didn't know you'd been back to see her.'

'Yes, I went on Monday, the day you started back at the boutique,' Gillian said by way of explanation.

'Working again, Holly?' Frank said quickly.

'No! Well, only helping out—behind the counter. Nothing else.' Holly seemed to emphasise the last two words.

'I hope you will be able to work again soon. I mean, real work, of course, Holly. I heard you'd been involved in another car accident. Dear me, you are careless.'

Holly was as tense as a taut string.

'Shall we continue our walk, Holly?' Gillian

urged the girl, a hand under her arm.

'How are you enjoying being at the cottage, Mrs Parker?' Frank Reynolds deliberately blocked their path.

'Gillian is helping with Chris,' Holly said quickly.

Frank Reynolds' expression underwent a subtle change. 'How is the kid? Has he said anything yet?'

Gillian felt a sudden urge to slap this man.

'Nothing,' Holly muttered.

'We'll be going back now, Holly,' Gillian said firmly. 'It's getting late.'

'Goodbye,' she said pointedly to Frank Reynolds.

'Oh, just good night, Mrs Parker. We'll meet again, as I said before.'

Gillian positively grabbed Holly's arm and pulled her back along the path the way they'd come. The meeting with Frank Reynolds was still horribly vivid in her mind.

She was certain it had not been accidental. Holly knew he would be there and for some reason she wanted Gillian along. Perhaps this meeting had been arranged when Holly had been on the telephone earlier. But Gillian was just as certain that Frank hadn't expected her to be there. It had seemed to her, too, that every sentence exchanged between the two held a subtler meaning than she was able to divine.

'Were you involved in the same accident as Roy's wife?' she asked.

91

The girl's eyes were wide with fear.

'No, no, you mustn't say that. How could I be there? I was just looking after Chris, wasn't I? Frank just meant another car accident in the family.'

'He seems to have known Carol very well,' Gillian said.

'That's gossip.' Holly's voice was higher now. 'You mustn't listen. I suppose Barbara Reynolds told you. She would be trying to make you stop thinking about her and James—'

Holly caught her breath. 'Sorry, Gillian.'

'Barbara said nothing about Carol, but Frank did.'

'What did he say? What did he say?' Holly was clearly becoming hysterical.

'Just that he knew her quite well.' Gillian paused a moment. 'Does Roy like Frank?'

'No! You mustn't tell Roy we met him tonight. Promise me, Gillian, promise me!' Holly was sobbing now.

Gillian put an arm round the frightened girl.

'I promise. Now calm down, we'll have to go in. We're home.'

She saw that Holly had some cocoa and went straight up to bed. Later, she sat in the living-room, a magazine in front of her, but she didn't read a word. Her head was buzzing with that barbed, meaningful conversation between Holly and Frank.

Knowing so little of Holly's life before the

accident, Gillian couldn't hope to unravel what the two had meant, but one fact stood out clearly. There was something unexplained about Carol's car accident. Something Holly didn't want Roy to know—and was frightened he would find out.

Roy was sitting opposite Gillian, working on some papers which were strewn all over the coffee table. He looked relaxed, as if he was enjoying his work.

Dare she broach the subject of the accident with him? Would she only be opening up scarcely-healed wounds? His wife's death must have been a terrible shock to him, and to Chris. Then she remembered Frank asking about Chris. Why should he be important to him?

If only she knew exactly what had happened on that day. Was there no one else to ask? Someone she knew?

Of course there was someone—Barbara Reynolds. She was a local girl—but she was the last person Gillian felt like confiding in!

Roy looked up suddenly, catching her unawares.

'You're very pensive. Not tired I hope?' He sounded concerned.

'No, not at all,' she said quickly. 'Would you like some tea?'

'Yes, please,' he said with a smile.

She rose. She had been wrong. Roy was now treating her in a friendly fashion, almost like one of the family. It certainly made for a much pleasanter atmosphere. Perhaps his antagonism hadn't been directed at her, just at circumstances.

As she walked through the hall, her thoughts returned to Frank Reynolds. Maybe she should make some quiet inquiries. The telephone rang suddenly by her side.

'Can you get it please, Gillian? If I move now, I'll lose my place,' Roy called.

'Sure,' she answered and lifted the receiver, giving the number.

'Hello, that is Gillian, isn't it?' the voice said at the other end. 'This is James.'

CHAPTER FIVE

Gillian automatically filled the kettle, her thoughts full of her telephone conversation with James.

Not that they had really said much to each other, beyond making arrangements to meet.

She realised she was thinking more of her reaction to speaking to him for the first time in months.

Her heart had leapt when she first heard his voice, but she had felt strangely calm during the conversation. She was surprised that it was so difficult to analyse her feelings towards him now.

She knew she'd loved him when he left her

94

because she'd felt terrible pain. Since then, somehow, it had gradually lessened. That, of course, could be due to the fact that she'd had so much to think about. In fact, more had happened to her in the last few weeks, it seemed, than in all of their eight years of marriage.

'I take it that was your husband on the phone?'

She jumped at the sound of Roy's voice behind her.

'Yes.' She turned and smiled at him, suddenly noticing, at the same time, that the kettle was boiling over.

'Oh, dear, I forgot.' She reached over.

'No.' Roy's hand came out to stay hers. 'I'll make the tea. Go and sit down.'

He came into the sitting-room a few minutes later with a tray of tea and biscuits.

'Cups and saucers.' He smiled, pointing at the tray. 'I've become quite civilised again since you came.'

'Gillian,' Roy began hesitantly. 'Your private life is your own business and I don't want to pry, but if you want to leave, I'll understand. However, I'll be very sorry to see you go.'

'I don't know if I'm going or not. James didn't say anything that—'

She paused, then said honestly, 'I don't even know what I want, Roy.'

'You mean that, even if James wants to

95

patch up your marriage, you're not sure?'

'The first time I came to Harbury I wanted only one thing—to be with James again and to return to our former way of life. It was only after I got home that I wondered, for the first time, if that's actually what had been wrong— our former way of life.

'Now, my own life is so changed, and I think I am gradually changing, too. I'm no longer the clinging person James left.'

Roy ran his fingers through his hair. 'You know, Gillian, whatever you decide, I owe you an apology.'

He looked at her briefly. 'I've been selfish, asking you to come here to help me with Chris and Holly.'

'But you're paying me,' she pointed out.

'That's just to salve my conscience. What you're doing here is far more than house-keeping. I could sense the difference in the three of us when you were last here. It didn't need much pushing on Holly's part for me to ask you to come back.'

'You can surely see I like being here. So, there's no need to feel guilty!' she said simply. 'Although, I must admit, it still puzzles me why Holly wanted me as a friend.'

'It puzzles me, too. You're complete opposites!' Roy grinned. 'Mind you, you're all the things Holly should be—responsible, sensible and thoughtful.'

'She's very young,' Gillian pointed out in

Holly's defence.

'Yes,' he admitted. 'And insecure. I seem to have alternately spoiled her and neglected her. Our parents died when she was only sixteen. Just at the most vulnerable and, I suppose, emotional time of her life.

'I was twenty-six, rather immersed in my career and without a clue about coping with a teenager. She was artistic and seemed to have a flair for design. So, within a year, I found her a place at art school. She's a silver-smith by profession, actually.'

'Really! I had no idea,' Gillian exclaimed, impressed. 'I'd love to see some of her work.'

'She hasn't made anything for a long time,' Roy said. 'Not—not since Carol's accident.'

There was a silence and, after a moment, he continued.

'It was at art school that she and Carol met. Holly was drawn to her like a moth to a candle.'

He paused, and added, almost too quietly for Gillian to hear, 'As I was.'

'Carol painted.' He half-turned in the chair and pointed to a framed oil painting on the wall behind him. 'That's an example of her work.'

It was a still life of a bowl of anemonies, the colours velvety and rich and the background a shimmer of silk. It was very beautiful.

'It's a work of art, and I mean that in its most truthful way,' Gillian said.

'Yes, she was brilliant,' Roy conceded briefly. 'And she certainly shook us out of our well-ordered, but rather lonely lives. I still remember that first week-end Holly brought her home to meet me.'

He was silent for a while and Gillian remained quiet, not wanting to intrude on delicate memories.

'I was the wrong husband for Carol,' he continued after a while. 'I was too old-fashioned. I assumed she would give up her parties and casual way of life, once we were married. Holly couldn't see my point of view either. In her eyes, Carol could do no wrong. Maybe it was my fault.'

Gillian looked at him with concern. He really believed he had been in the wrong. Surely, though, it took two to break up a marriage?

She knew within herself now that James would never have gone to Barbara, if something hadn't been missing in their own marriage. Something she reasoned now, that she had omitted to put into it, just as much as James.

'Chris was born within a year of our marriage,' Roy told her. 'Carol loved him, but she hadn't the slightest idea of training or discipline, that was totally foreign to her nature. Anyway, where Chris was concerned, all that was left to me. No wonder the little chap is scared of me,' he finished ruefully.

'I think he's getting to know you better now.' Gillian's voice was gentle.

'Yes, it's beginning to look that way,' Roy said carefully, but she could still detect the hope in his voice.

'Unfortunately, my job took me abroad when Chris was a toddler and Carol wouldn't come. I couldn't take Chris away from her, so our marriage limped along. Holly stayed here with Carol and Chris.

'I'm not sure now if that was a good idea. For one thing, she met Frank Reynolds. If I'd been at home, I would have put a stop to that relationship very quickly.'

He grimaced at Gillian. 'I can't pin anything on him, but I just don't like him.'

'Neither do I.'

'I didn't know you'd met him.' Roy sounded astonished.

'He was at the hotel when I went to speak with his sister.'

'I see.'

*   *   *

Gillian suddenly decided that she might not have been helping Holly at all when she'd concealed their previous meeting with Reynolds from Roy.

'I also met him this evening. When Holly and I went for a walk.'

Roy looked at her sharply. 'Do you mean

99

Holly's still seeing him?' he demanded.

'I had the feeling that Frank expected to meet Holly, that perhaps it had been arranged. I'm equally certain Holly wanted me there. Although I can't think why.' Roy stared at his linked hands for a moment.

'Tell me, Gillian, that first day you met her at the Eidelweiss ... was she with Frank then?'

'I didn't actually meet Holly then. I was aware of a girl hovering in the background of the reception area. The first time I really saw her, however, was when she ran out—' She stopped, remembering Holly's insinuation that the accident had been Gillian's fault.

'You don't think she wanted you to hit her?' he whispered.

'No, never,' Gillian said firmly. 'She just meant to attract my attention.'

Roy passed a hand over his eyes. 'It's haunted me since your accident—that I might have driven her to do something desperate. You see, I'd forbidden her to see Frank. He seems to have some kind of fascination for her.

'To be truthful, she's never recovered from Carol's death. She hasn't taken an interest in anything, not even her work. She wasn't even keen to start work at the boutique again. I began to think that by forbidding her to see Frank, I might have destroyed the last thing she cared about, and she wanted to take her own life.'

'It wasn't like that,' Gillian assured him.

'She just misjudged how near I was to her. I'm glad you know the accident was not my fault.'

Roy leaned forward and put a hand on hers.

'I hated myself for behaving like that towards you, accusing you. I really wanted to think that you had been responsible—the alternative was too awful to even consider. Can you forgive me for that, Gillian?'

'Yes, of course,' she said softly. 'I'm glad I know why now. Yet, I was sure you couldn't think I'd be so irresponsible.'

'I never was very good at saying sorry. It isn't so difficult now that I know you better. Mind you, I'd thought I'd done it in a roundabout way by giving you my car and asking you to drive Chris and Holly around.' He grinned sheepishly.

She laughed softly. 'Well, it did occur to me that you couldn't think too badly of my driving.'

They sat for a few moments more, just smiling and looking at each other.

'Whatever happens in the future, Gillian, you know you have friends here. Chris and Holly . . . and me.'

'Yes,' she said softly. 'I know.'

As she climbed into bed later, she reflected how dangerous it was to take people at face value or make instant judgments.

Holly's petulance was obviously entirely due to insecurity and a need to find someone to identify with. Her first choice, Carol, was gone

101

now, and Holly was adrift. Perhaps Holly saw her, Gillian, as a second choice. Perhaps, that was why she'd asked for help that day on the road.

What about Roy? That brusque, off-hand manner was not really a part of his personality, but the result of all the pressures on him.

People are a little like icebergs, she thought. Only about one tenth of their personality showing. Perhaps, too, she didn't know all about James—even after eight years.

*   *   *

The following day, she seemed possessed of a new, driving energy, and the housework was completed in record time.

One room she hadn't yet ventured to clean was Roy's study. She had hesitated before, as he hadn't mentioned it, and she thought it might be an invasion of privacy. But now, since their long chat last night, she no longer felt an outsider in the Andrews family. With Roy being so open and frank about his situation, she realised he would have no objection now.

Her attention was arrested by a painting on the study wall. It was a familiar painting. She walked closer to it. It was an oil painting of a mountain scene, signed by an artist whose name was vaguely familiar to her.

She stared, puzzled. Surely this painting was the twin of the one in Barbara Reynolds' office

102

at the Eidelweiss? But that couldn't be. Barbara's was an oil painting, too. Gillian shrugged. Perhaps she was mistaken.

Chris, too, seemed to be in a lighthearted mood when she picked him up from school. He answered her questions with bright nods and shakes of his head.

'What story did you have today in class?' she asked, as they turned into the cottage drive.

He waited until they were out of the car, then flapped his arms up and down like wings.

'A story about birds?'

He shook his head.

'Aeroplanes?'

He grinned widely and again shook his head.

No matter how he mimed, Gillian just could not guess the story. Eventually Chris dragged some paper from his schoolbag and began to draw. Gillian looked on, puzzled. That looked like a stage!

'Was it a play?'

He clapped his hands.

Her throat constricted. Had the teacher coaxed him to speak!

'Did—did you have a part?' she asked warily.

Again he drew. This time it was a crocodile with an alarm clock in its mouth. Suddenly, everything fell into place.

'The play was "Peter Pan" and you had the part of the crocodile?'

Chris grinned triumphantly.

103

Gillian strove hard to keep the excitement from showing in her face. She wasn't going to ask him any more at the moment.

She felt they were so near a break-through in encouraging Chris to talk again. She wanted Roy, though, to be the one to hear the first word. And even though he didn't speak just yet, the fact that he was drawing answers to questions, would soon make Roy aware of Chris's ability and talent.

*   *   *

Later, as soon as dinner was cleared away, she turned to Roy.

'Chris had a part in "Peter Pan" today. Wasn't that exciting?'

Roy turned to his son. 'Really?' Astonishment was mixed with hope in his expression. 'Which part did you play?'

Unobtrusively, Gillian pushed paper and pencil across the table to Chris. She knew he'd seen her do it, but he ignored it and got down on the floor and mimed a crocodile. He'd taken the wooden salt and pepper mills from the table and clicked them together rather like castanets to give them the sound of the alarm clock ticking.

Roy roared with laughter, grabbed the soup ladle, pushed its handle up his sleeve and covered his hand with the bowl.

'I'm Captain Hook!' he shouted, and began

chasing a delighted Chris round the room.

Gillian slipped out of the kitchen. Why wouldn't Chris draw for his father? That was the second time he'd avoided doing so. She must get to the bottom of it.

It was time, however, to leave for the Eidelweiss, so Gillian dressed with care. The meeting with James had been in her mind all day and she was nervous and apprehensive. As she left her room, Roy came out of Chris's bedroom. He looked happy.

'I really believe things have taken a turn for the better,' he said, referring to Chris.

'He's artistic you know, Roy. Perhaps he may even be an artist like your wife.'

'You saw that drawing of the bluebell he did. He hasn't a bit of talent. I can't say I'm sorry. I'd hate to think he'd turn out like—' He stopped abruptly.

It was a point of view that hadn't occurred to Gillian. Quickly, she tried to think of something else to say.

'That's a good oil painting in your study. I see your wife isn't the artist, though.'

'No, that's an original by some Dutch painter. Carol and I bought it at an auction just after we married. It's a bit sombre for my taste, but I gather it's worth a great deal.'

They walked to the door together. He looked at her with concern and she could tell he didn't know what to say.

'I'll have some tea waiting when you come

back,' he said a little lamely.

She smiled her thanks and left the cottage. She took the path from Roy's cottage, which led her past the spot where she'd had the accident with Holly. Gillian had admitted to Roy that she thought Holly was trying to attract her attention that day, but neither of them had questioned why Holly had need of a total stranger.

However, now was not the time for her to puzzle that out. She was nervous and apprehensive about meeting James again.

To her surprise, he was waiting for her by one of the small staff bungalows behind the hotel. Even from a distance, she could detect a tenseness about his solid, stocky figure. His smile was tentative and uncertain.

'Hello, James,' she said, her voice steady, even though her heart was racing.

'Gillian.' He nodded. 'Good to see you again. I thought we could have a chat in here. It will be more private.'

He ushered her into the first bungalow. She realised it must be Barbara's. It was pleasantly, if unimaginatively furnished, with some antique pieces. She wasn't really interested in her surroundings, however.

'How are you, James?' she asked, noting with surprise that he'd put on some weight.

'I've had a bad time,' he said, a little defensively. 'It started off as an ordinary cold, then I had symptoms of flu. Pneumonia developed from that. The doctor said I needed a good rest,' he finished ponderously.

'Yes—well you've had that,' she replied briskly. James had always tended to take his ailments very seriously.

'I'm completely over it now, I'm glad to say. As I said on the phone to you, I'm back at work again.'

'Harbury is now your permanent base then?' It was a rather pointed question, but she knew they must start somewhere and guessed she would have to take the initiative.

James looked uncomfortable. 'Well, yes. The opportunity of a transfer came up, and I took it.'

'You were going to tell me, sometime, I take it?' she asked simply.

'I was going to ask you if you'd like to come here to live,' he replied stiffly.

'Were you?'

He wriggled in his chair. 'I wasn't going to just abandon you!' he protested.

'You wanted me to come here. To live with you?' she probed gently.

'I didn't know if you'd want to live with me again,' he said slowly.

'But did you want me?' she persisted.

'Well, you're my wife. Though, I wasn't sure if you still wanted...' His eyes fell from her gaze and he slumped down in the chair again.

'I can't believe that you would want to leave Barbara,' she said. 'Not now.'

He put his face in his hands. 'Believe me, we never meant that to happen. Never. We can't let the child cloud the issue though. My duty is to you.'

'No, James, we're past talking about duty. We're talking now about need, and Barbara certainly needs you. And I think you need her.'

'Gillian, what about you?' he asked, his round face crumpled with anxiety.

Yes, indeed, what about her?

Gillian knew that she needed someone just as much as anyone else. She'd needed James all those months he'd been away, and yet he'd not once asked how she'd managed to cope or how things were in Banford. She'd needed James and yet she'd survived. She hadn't cracked up.

'I've changed, James,' she said, knowing that what she said now would decide their futures. 'I don't mean I'm bitter and envious. It's just that I've become more independent.'

Still he said nothing. He simply sat, watching her.

'We've had a good marriage, but ... but maybe we've grown too far apart to continue.'

*   *   *

The relief on his face was enormous, and Gillian felt torn in two with hurt.

He hadn't wanted her back at all. That was obvious. He just hadn't had the courage to make the decision. How long would he have

108

avoided the issue, if she hadn't made the first move? How long would he have allowed her to drift on with her life, not knowing the future? She was quite sure he had no idea how cruel he had been.

'I'll see that you're not short of money,' he began.

'Never mind that, James.' Her irritation with him made her abrupt. 'I have a job.'

'Oh, yes, I heard about that. When do you go back to Mr Hunter?'

'He sold out. I was made redundant.'

'I didn't know that.'

'It has been five months since we spoke,' she said tartly.

James's bland face flushed and he mumbled some kind of apology.

'Can I leave you to find a lawyer to handle the divorce?' she asked.

She saw his head come up and she was surprised at the way the word had come off her tongue. Divorce was something that happened to other people. There was no going back now, however.

'Yes, I'll see to all that.' He paused for a moment. 'Gillian, you've been marvellous about this. You could have made it nasty—'

'There's no point in that,' she said briskly. She didn't want recriminations or regret. People said too many hurtful things when they were upset.

'I hope you'll still think of me with ... with

friendship,' James said.

She smiled a little to herself. He wanted it all ways. Still, she had nothing to lose. Her future was uncertain and she might well have to call on James for help of some kind for a while.

'Shall I walk you back to ... to wherever it is you're living?'

'No!' She felt rather disgusted with him and his show of concern. Hadn't he even bothered to find out exactly where she'd been living?

'We'll have to make arrangements about selling the house. I don't want to live there now. Call me if there's anything I have to sign. Good-night.'

She walked back along the woodland path feeling curiously detached from everything. She seemed to be divorced in thought from James already. He wanted his life cosy and uncomplicated, and if things didn't turn out that way he retreated from life.

Involuntarily, she thought of Roy whose life couldn't be more complicated and unhappy, but who was fighting every inch of the way to save his family. You had to admire a man like Roy Andrews.

Roy took a long, hard look at her when she returned and he was quick to assess her feelings. He didn't ask her anything, just handed her a brandy and said quietly, 'Drink that. It'll calm you, and see that you have a good night's sleep.'

'Well, you're stuck with me for the time

being,' she eventually said, as lightly as she could.

Roy looked at her steadily. 'As long as you made the right decision for you.'

'Yes, I'm sure it was the right thing for both of us. We'd drifted too far apart. It's just going to take some getting used to.'

As she rose to go, Roy laid a gentle arm round her shoulder.

'Sleep well.'

She was more touched by Roy's genuine concern, she realised, than by all James's assurances about financial help and friendship.

*   *   *

In the days that followed, Gillian found her involvement with the Andrews family was a balm to her hurt.

After some time, though, it dawned on her that she was suffering from hurt pride more than anything. Enough had happened to her in the last few months to make her realise that life was too short to dwell on a surface emotion. She began to think positively about her future. The solution came to her quite simply and naturally, and she felt happier than she had for many months.

Roy noticed the change in her.

'You're looking better this evening,' he said to her, about a week after her meeting with James.

111

She nodded. 'I've realised there is still quite a lot I want to do with my life.

'I'm going to take a refresher course in nursing.'

He frowned slightly. 'Soon?'

'Oh, no, not yet. I won't leave here while you need me,' she assured him.

'Good.' He spoke quietly. It was obvious he was relieved.

She had an appointment to see James the next day, so she decided to take the opportunity to speak to Barbara about her brother and ask her to see that he left Holly alone. She wanted so much to help Roy and his family.

This time, James was waiting for her in the Eidelweiss office. They had an unemotional and business-like discussion about the house and dividing their possessions. James was very fair and generous, and Gillian knew he'd realised how much he'd hurt her.

All through their chat, though, she was aware of the painting on the wall, the one that was so similar to Roy's. When they'd finished speaking, she went over to look at it. It was identical, even to the signature, but how could that be?

Just then, Barbara came in. She was edgy and prickly with Gillian. She realised the girl was obviously embarrassed, and so she tried to be as friendly as possible.

'I've been admiring your painting. Is it an

112

original?'

Barbara glanced quickly at the mountain scene.

'Yes, of course. I bought it from my brother. As I told you, he has an antique business. That cost me a fortune.'

Barbara fingered the heavy bird brooch Gillian had seen twice before. 'I bought this from him, too. He wouldn't touch reproductions!'

'Oh, yes your brother, Frank,' Gillian said, seizing on the opportunity of asking Barbara something about Carol's accident. 'I believe he knows Holly Andrews. And Carol Andrews. How well did he know her?'

Barbara's face tightened. 'I thought it was too good to be true. You agreed to give James a divorce too quickly, too easily. I knew there had to be a catch. You've come back to rake up scandal, haven't you? To drag the Reynolds' name in the dirt!'

With that, she turned and ran out of the office.

Gillian's confidence, optimism, and sense of well-being evaporated instantly. There was obviously something ugly in the past, something to do with Frank and Carol Andrews. The last thing she had wanted was to antagonise Barbara. Now, she might never learn the truth.

Angry at her own clumsiness, she turned to explain to James, but disgust was evident

113

in his face.

'That was a cheap way to get revenge,' he said bitterly. 'Just stay away from the Eidelweiss in future!'

CHAPTER SIX

'Well, well—the cast-off wife. How are you today?'

The arrogant figure of Frank Reynolds barred Gillian's escape from the Eidelweiss Hotel.

'If there was a reply to that I couldn't even be bothered to make it,' she said tightly. 'Excuse me!'

'Come now, not so quickly. You'll give the hotel a bad name.'

'What do you mean?'

'First, my sister rushes out of her office, to be followed by—We can't really call him your husband any longer. Shall we say Barbara's fiancé?' He paused, fractionally. 'Then you sidle out as if your fingers had been in the till.'

'I beg your pardon!'

Frank Reynolds shrugged. 'You looked guilty, Mrs Parker. I don't think it was because of anything you've done. I think it was something you said.'

'Who cares what you think?' Gillian said sharply. 'You weren't a fly on the wall in the office.' Her look said he had the same significance for her.

His expression darkened.

'Just give Miss Holly Andrews a message. Tell her I'm waiting for a little bird. She'll understand.' With a light agile movement he stepped aside.

Without an answer, Gillian walked straight out of the hotel.

Frank Reynolds was nothing more than a bully and obviously using her to threaten Holly. Had he bullied Carol Andrews, too? Gillian knew Roy suspected that there had been some kind of relationship between Holly and Frank, but she was certain he was not aware of the extent of that involvement.

Barbara and James had been upset by her inquiry, which she regretted, but she suspected that Barbara's use of the word 'scandal' was more dramatic than accurate. Scandal suggested public knowledge, and then it was usually inevitable that some well-meaning individual told the injured party—in this case Roy, and he knew nothing.

Therefore, whatever had happened was known to only a few people—Holly, Frank, Barbara and Carol. No doubt, too, James had now learned the details from Barbara. But it was useless to approach him as he would say nothing, to avoid upsetting Barbara.

Holly, then, was her only hope of getting at the truth.

Gillian hurried along the woodland path that led from the hotel to Roy's cottage. Today was Holly's half-day, so perhaps they could have an open conversation before Roy and Chris returned home.

She took her time approaching Holly on the subject. She baked some scones and made some coffee and quite deliberately lulled Holly into a comfortable and relaxed frame of mind.

'Roy tells me you are a silver-smith,' she began. 'I'd no idea you were so talented.'

'I did some silver work once,' the girl answered carelessly. 'I don't do anything in that line now.'

'Why ever not?'

Holly shrugged. 'I ran out of ideas for designs. I didn't have much talent in that direction.'

It was a glib, evasive answer, Gillian thought, as Holly quickly changed the subject.

'These scones are good. What's in them? Cheese? You really must teach me to bake.'

'Were you in love with Frank Reynolds?' Gillian asked abruptly, using Holly's own tactics.

Holly laughed, shortly and bitterly. 'Never.'

'Was Carol?'

The scone crumbled in Holly's hand.

'You've no right to ask that. It's none of your business.'

'I'm not asking out of idle curiosity. Or mere gossip. Frank Reynolds hinted as much to me.'

116

'Damn the man!' Holly muttered. 'Don't ever tell Roy what he said. In fact, don't ever mention that man to Roy.'

She looked at Gillian intensely for a moment, then relaxed a little.

'Even the suggestion that Carol was interested in someone else would kill Roy—he adored Carol. I doubt if he'll ever get over her death. Promise me you'll never mention Frank to him.'

Holly's eyes were open wide as if to impress her honesty on Gillian. But the tone of the last few sentences had sounded false. She had the impression that Holly was trying to shift the point. Besides, she was lying. Roy had frankly told Gillian how shaky his marriage had been for years and, since Holly had lived with them all their married life, it must have been obvious to her.

Nevertheless, she wouldn't dream of hurting Roy unnecessarily. There was no need for him to know anything about an association between Carol and Frank. Gillian wasn't quite ready, however, to abandon the subject completely.

'Surely it would be better for Roy to know the truth than to have this false image of his wife?'

'Gillian, I've asked you!' Holly's voice was strident, touching on an hysterical note. 'Don't ever mention Frank Reynolds to Roy in any context.'

117

'Sorry.' Gillian lightly touched the girl's arm. 'I guess I just can't stand the man, but I respect your wishes. Now, let's go see some of your silver work.'

It was a bit of an underhand trick, and Holly fell for it.

'Yes, O K.' She was desperate to end the conversation about Frank, as Gillian had guessed.

Upstairs in her bedroom, Holly took a velvet bag from her dressing-table drawer and shook out an assortment of rings and necklaces on to her bedspread. She was off-hand in her manner.

'I've sold the best.'

Gillian picked up the jewellery and tried on one or two rings, hiding her disappointment. They were pretty, beautifully made, but there was no originality in their designs.

'These are well made,' she commented, examining a small, neat ring.

'Do you really think so?'

There was a desperate appeal for admiration in that girlish voice. Gillian realised she had touched on another aspect of Holly's insecurity.

'Please have one,' Holly said.

'That's not why I asked to see them!'

'I know, but it would mean something to me if you would wear one of my pieces. Please?'

'Well—'

'I have some brooches. You might prefer

118

one of those.' She jumped off the bed and began scrabbling in her drawer.

Gillian put the rings and necklaces back in the velvet bag and took it over to join Holly. There were some brooches fashioned after horses and rabbits; there was an owl and a swan, but at the back of the drawer she saw a brooch that looked familiar.

'That one, Holly—at the back. It's a bird of some kind.'

Holly snatched at the bird brooch and slipped it into her pocket. 'I can't let you have that one.' Her voice was shaky again. 'Not one of my best efforts. Totally unrecognisable bird.'

It wasn't unrecognisable to Gillian, however. It was the exact duplicate of the antique silver brooch worn by Barbara Reynolds.

It wasn't a copy of a real bird, more a fantasy design, with its hawk-like head, long, narrow breast and square-tipped wing feathers. Yet Barbara had told Gillian quite clearly that Frank had sold her the brooch and that it was an original. 'Frank wouldn't touch reproductions,' had been Barbara's very words.

She could sense Holly was still upset.

'Actually, Holly, I'd be proud to wear something you'd made. May I have that little plaited silver ring?'

Gillian smoothed over the moment

119

beautifully and with absolute truth. She was fond of Holly and would be proud to display something of hers.

* * *

Her thoughts were anything but smooth, though, as she drove to collect Chris from school. If Holly had made that bird brooch, then it could be assumed that she had made the other, too.

Gillian had deliberately not given her Frank's message. 'Tell her I'm waiting for a little bird.' Surely that must refer to the brooch? Could it be that Holly made those and Frank sold them as antique jewellery?

Then, too, there was the coincidence of the identical paintings. The one in Roy's study and its twin in Barbara's office—the one she'd told Gillian had cost her a fortune when she bought it from Frank.

How many were there of those? Obviously, Frank could only sell one of each item here in Harbury, so he must have other outlets.

The whole thing sounded absolutely fantastic, and Gillian wondered if she'd let her imagination run away with her completely. She had heard of people faking antiques, but surely there was some way of identification?

Perhaps she could go to the library and do some reading on the subject. Then she remembered Sue Jackson, her next door neighbour in Banford, had been crazy about old things. Sue had gone to auctions and house sales and surely must have picked up a fair amount of knowledge.

Gillian parked outside the school gates, a small smile on her face. She knew exactly what she was going to do. She was going to buy an antique from Frank Reynolds.

In the event, it proved to be a very simple thing to do, and served two purposes. She had been uneasy about the strained relationship between Barbara, James and herself, and she knew she had to remedy that.

When she arrived at the hotel next day, Barbara was behind the reception desk.

'I've come to apologise,' Gillian said at once.

'I said something the other day which sounded offensive. It wasn't meant like that at all. I was just curious to know if Carol Andrews had bought some antique pieces from your brother.'

Barbara looked slightly mollified but her stiff manner didn't unbend.

'Quite possibly. I know she and Frank went to auctions together. She gave him her opinion of the art work on sale.'

'I see. There are one or two nice pieces in Roy Andrews' house and I assumed Carol had bought them from Skua Antiques.'

Casually, she wandered over to the showcases. 'I've always been fascinated by old silver. That bangle is really beautiful.' She

121

pointed to a heavy silver bangle, intricately engraved. 'Is your brother here?'

'He's away for a couple of days, seeing some dealers.' Barbara took a key from her desk and came over to the show-case. 'I have a list of prices, so if you really want to buy it—'

Gillian slipped the bangle over her wrist. 'Oh, I do, I do.'

She almost changed her mind when Barbara stated the price; it was astronomical. Since it was the only safe way of probing into Frank's dealings however, she had to buy it.

'I'll tell James you called.' Barbara's voice was warmer now, as she wrapped the bangle.

'Please do.' Gillian smiled at her, knowing the girl would tell James that she hadn't been out to cause trouble after all.

It was obvious that Barbara hadn't the slightest idea that her brother was involved in faking antiques, if indeed that was what he was doing.

Gillian went straight home, parcelled the bangle, enclosed a note to Sue and hurried to the post office. She would soon know if her suspicions were correct. She remembered now that all silver carried hallmarks, giving dates of manufacture and other details. He could hardly fake those.

* * *

Next day was Saturday, and when she arrived

122

home after shopping, she found Roy and Chris waiting for her with a prepared picnic basket.

'It's the week-end—time to enjoy ourselves,' Roy told her. 'Slip into some jeans and a warm sweater and prepare for exercise!'

'Give me five minutes.' She raced upstairs.

When she came down again, Roy was waiting with her cord jacket and he placed it across her shoulders.

'Chris did the sandwiches. I made the coffee. We have bags of apples and nuts. What more could you ask?'

'How clever of you both.' Gillian laughed. 'Where are we going?'

Chris pointed to the north.

'Right up over the moors,' Roy told her. 'Time you saw some of this breath-taking country we live in.'

There was no sign of Holly and Gillian took it that once again she'd decided not to join in a family outing.

Once they were clear of the woods, the dog streaked ahead, disappearing for minutes in clumps of ferns and gorse. They followed it and it seemed the most natural thing in the world when Chris took Gillian's hand and then his father's, and, linked together, they set out over the moors.

Gillian was aware of Roy's head turning towards her. As their eyes met over the child's head, she could see the happiness written all over his face at Chris's spontaneous gesture.

Why, we're almost like a little family, she thought involuntarily. In that instant, she realised that Roy had had the same thought.

There was something else too in his expression as he looked at her, something for her alone. She smiled slightly. She knew he was grateful to her for helping with Chris.

The day was a great success. They played rounders and pig-in-the-middle and ate the huge, untidy sandwiches that Chris had lovingly made.

'What shall we do now?' Roy asked Chris as they finished packing the empty flasks and wrappers in the picnic basket.

The boy stood before them, his eyes seemed darker by the intensity of their expression. Both Roy and Gillian realised that he was trying to speak to them.

They sat, not daring to say anything or even to move, but unable to tear their eyes from the mouth trying so desperately to form words. It was too much for him. With a shrug, he turned and ran off, chasing the dog.

Roy said nothing at first, then turned to Gillian.

'We're nearly there.' His voice was quiet. 'I think he nearly made it that time, Gill.'

'We mustn't rush it.'

'I know, I know.' He nodded. 'I always used to think that another shock would release his tongue, but now it looks as if a happy, relaxed moment might be the key.'

'Was it the shock of his mother's death that caused him to lose his speech?'

There was a long silence.

'That's the medical opinion,' he said eventually. 'But I'm not sure. Certainly he hasn't spoken from that time, but, somehow, I feel as if it has more to do with me.'

'Weren't you abroad when—'

He nodded. 'Yes, and he was unable to speak even before I came home. It's just that I've always wondered if Chris thinks Carol might be alive if I had not been away from home.'

He shrugged. 'I've tried to think of it from all angles, because at first when I came home, he wouldn't even look at me. He seemed to want to avoid me.'

'Perhaps he was so wrapped up in his own unhappiness. Has Holly been unable to help him?'

'She hasn't tried,' Roy said bluntly. 'I know she's fond of Chris, but she doesn't seem to have made any special effort. Not like you.'

She smiled. 'I'm new to Chris. Our friendship has nothing to do with the past. Perhaps it's easier for him to be natural with me.'

'There's so much of the world we could explore together.' Roy gazed out over the moor watching the figure of his son as he leapt from tussock to tussock, the dog chasing at his heels.

125

They had missed so much, those two, Gillian thought.

'Will you work abroad again?'

'No, I don't think so,' he said. 'Chris needs a settled home for a while.' He paused for a moment. 'I'm content here now.'

*   *   *

Shortly after, the sky began to darken, and they made their way home.

They toasted scones and sat round the fire. Roy brought out a book about early aircraft and he and Chris pored over the pictures, as they sat side by side on the sofa.

After a while, Chris indicated that he was going upstairs. He returned with a large scrapbook which he shyly offered to Roy.

Gillian noticed his father's look of amazement at the many pictures of aircraft that Chris had cut from newspapers and magazines and pasted into his book. With great glee, they compared pictures from the glossy coffee table book with those in the scruffy, dogeared scrapbook.

She leaned back in her chair, totally relaxed, reflecting this was the most perfect day there had been since she'd come to Harbury. Every minute seemed to bring Roy and Chris closer together.

Then, as Chris turned another page in his book, a piece of paper fluttered on to the floor.

126

All three bent to look, expecting to see a vintage aeroplane.

Then with a feeling of inexplicable apprehension, Gillian saw it was a drawing. A drawing of a bird with a falcon's head, long narrow breast and square tips to its wing feathers.

'Hey, that's unusual. Did you draw this, Chris?' Roy held the drawing between forefinger and thumb.

When Gillian looked at Chris, his face was white and rigid. He had noticed that she recognised the drawing. He turned to his father, shaking his head and backing out of the room.

'Chris? What is it? Chris, come back!'

The boy fled from the room and they heard his feet clatter up the stairs, the sound of his bedroom door opening and slamming closed.

'Gill—what happened?' Roy was near breaking point.

He half-rose from his chair. 'He looked so scared of me. I'd better go up to him—'

'No,' she said with gentleness, putting her hand on his shoulder and urging him to sit down again. 'Let me try to explain.'

He looked at her in bewilderment.

'Did you ever say in Chris's company, without realising the implications, that you hoped he wouldn't turn out to be an artist, too? You said something like that to me once.'

He thought for a while. 'I don't know—I

might have done. Oh, Lord—'

He put his head in his hands. 'I remember now you hinted to me that he might be artistic.' He raised his head again. 'You mean he can draw—and is terrified of me knowing?'

She told him about the drawings of the bluebell, the first-rate one Chris had done for her, and reminded him of the crude one Chris had drawn in the forest.

'I think he might be afraid that you'd disapprove of his drawings.'

Roy's face was white and drawn. 'I'll go and explain.'

'May I see him first?' Gillian jumped to her feet. 'I'm not trying to intrude between you and your son, but he knows that I've seen his work before. If I tell him first, that you're not angry, just surprised, it may make it easier for you.'

'Thanks.' He nodded in agreement.

She hurried upstairs. She had a far more important reason for wanting to see Chris. What she'd said to Roy was true, but there was another problem he didn't suspect.

Chris was still scared.

'Your daddy doesn't know anything about the bird. Absolutely nothing,' she told him at once.

His eyes, large and fearful, stared at her.

'I only know because I saw a brooch which Holly had made. Did you draw the design for her?'

He nodded.

128

'And you don't want Daddy to know?'

He shook his head.

'But you don't mind him knowing about your other drawings?'

He smiled tentatively.

'Then that's fine.' She hugged him. 'Your daddy doesn't know anything about the brooch. So it will be just another drawing to him. It's all in the past now, isn't it?'

His face cleared and he smiled happily.

'He's going to be very proud when you show him all your other drawings.'

As she left Chris's room, she saw him take a sketch pad from under his mattress and slowly leaf through it. She had no idea what Roy would say to Chris, but she knew he would handle this whole crucial question with love and understanding. She knew enough of him to be sure of that.

Downstairs, she spoke briefly to Roy, then went to her bedroom. She was troubled. There was so much she was keeping from Roy, and yet to tell him would give him even more unhappiness.

For Chris to make a simple drawing for Holly seemed natural enough. For Holly to create a brooch from his design was also natural. Why then should the sight of this odd bird arouse such fear and panic in both of them?

Obviously, Chris had been warned not to tell his father. But by whom? By Holly? Why

129

should she do this to her own nephew?

Gillian lay back on her bed and thought about the girl and her attitude to Chris. It hadn't occurred to her before, but Holly took very little notice of him.

Never in all the time since she'd been living here, had Holly made any real effort to encourage Chris to speak. She hadn't played with him or taken the slightest interest. Didn't Holly want him to speak? Gillian was horrified by the thought.

There was no doubt now in Gillian's mind that Holly had been making 'antique' brooches for Frank. Had Carol been forging paintings for him, and had it all stopped with her death? Certainly, Roy had told her when she'd first come, that Holly hadn't worked since Carol's death.

It was obvious that Frank was trying to make Holly work for him again. And equally obvious that Holly didn't want to.

So why didn't she just refuse? It wasn't as if he could threaten her with exposure for what she'd already done, since he'd be found out, too.

Gillian had little sleep that night. Next day was Sunday and there was no opportunity to speak to Holly alone, but Gillian was happy to see that the discovery of the drawing had not damaged the fragile relationship between Roy and Chris. There was obviously no restraint between them.

Just after lunch, they heard the crunch of car tyres on the cottage drive.

'Visitors?' Roy went to the front door obviously surprised.

The others could tell by the formality of Roy's voice that strangers were on the door step, but Gillian was most surprised when she heard Mr Hunter's voice.

'It's Mr Hunter. I used to work for him in Banford,' she told Holly, then hurried out to the hall to greet him. To her added pleasure, his wife was with him.

Gillian hugged them both, then made the introductions. Roy ushered everyone into the sitting-room.

'We're on our way to Scotland,' Mr Hunter said, settling himself on the sofa. 'We decided before we left home that we were going to call and see Gillian. I hope you don't mind, Mr Andrews.'

'I'm delighted to meet Gillian's friends. We've taken up so much of her time, that she hasn't had an opportunity of visiting Banford yet,' Roy told him.

Over tea, the Hunters told them of all the places they'd visited recently and Gillian was secretly amused at how intrepid her old friends had become.

'If I may say so, you look years younger, Mr Hunter.' She laughed.

131

'And I used to think that life held nothing but work.' He shook his head.

'By the way, I have a letter for you, Gillian, from Sue Jackson. We've been keeping in touch and I told her we were calling to see you.'

He took a letter from his inside jacket pocket and passed it over.

Trying to be as nonchalant as possible, she slipped it into her skirt pocket, but her heart was racing and her fingers itched to tear open the envelope. This was one letter, though, she could only read in private.

Gillian was genuinely sorry when it was time for the Hunters to leave.

'Do call on your way back from Scotland,' Roy said, 'we'd like to meet you again.'

'We're off to Italy next month,' Mrs Hunter said. 'I'm rather worried, though, as we've never been abroad before. I would really like someone younger to come with us.'

Gillian knew at once that they intended inviting her, but she said nothing. She had no idea whether she would still be in Harbury in a month's time. One thing was sure, she wasn't leaving until Roy no longer had need of her.

'Italy is a wonderful country,' Holly said enthusiastically. 'I love it, particularly the art galleries and museums.'

Sad as she was to see them go, Gillian could hardly wait to open Sue's letter. She went up to her own room and with trembling fingers slit the envelope.

It was a long letter and her eyes skimmed over the felicitations and neighbourhood chat, until the word 'antique' leapt out of the paper. *'I checked out the bangle from reference books—no joy. Then I took it to Horseshoe Antiques, in Banford High Street. They say it seems genuine,* Sue wrote.

'I say "seems" because it wasn't made in this country—the silver marks are foreign, and there's no way their accuracy can be checked in this country. The Horseshoe man thinks it's probably Italian. It could be eighty to a hundred years old. Sorry I can't be more specific.

'What's going on anyway? I thought you had a little family job in Harbury, but your letter sounds so mysterious.'

Gillian flung down the letter. No proof! Oh, it was frustrating. Had Frank Reynolds stumbled on the perfect crime? There was only one way to be sure—to ask Holly.

Her opportunity came later in the day when Roy took Chris out to the garden to fly a kite they had made. Gillian went to Holly's room, knocked and went in without waiting for a reply.

'I forgot to give you a message from Frank Reynolds,' she said bleakly. 'He said, "Tell Holly I'm waiting for a little bird".'

Holly's laugh was high and strained. 'Stupid message. It means nothing to me.'

'Holly, don't do it.'

'What?'

133

'Make any more brooches.'

Holly stared at her.

'Barbara Reynolds has an identical brooch to the one in your drawer. The one you created from Chris's drawing.'

Holly didn't shout hysterically, as Gillian had expected, or even deny it. She just sat absolutely still and began to cry quite silently.

It was frightening—and chilling.

Gillian knelt by the girl. 'You don't have to make any more. He can't force you. He can't expose you since he's involved, too.'

The girl's weeping didn't cease.

'He has no hold over you, Holly!' Gillian persisted.

'But he has, he has!' Holly's voice shook through her sobs. 'It isn't only the jewellery, there's ... there's ...'

'What?'

The girl took her hands away from her tear-ravaged face.

'I killed Carol!'

CHAPTER SEVEN

It was some time before Gillian could calm Holly. All the time her heart grieved for her. Had she been carrying the guilt of the accident all that time? No wonder she was so moody and unpredictable.

134

Gillian could see she was in danger of going to pieces completely and realised that she must get her to tell the full story. If the burden of that was released, she might feel better.

Slowly, and with infinite patience and reassurance, she led Holly into the story.

'We'd been to a party the night before,' she began. 'Frank, Carol, and myself. We'd left Chris asleep at home, but I was worried about him and anxious to get back. I kept finishing off my drinks very quickly and saying it was time to go. I do remember that. Truly, I didn't want to stay, Gillian.'

'Of course. I understand.'

'I wasn't used to drinking a lot,' the girl continued. 'When we finally left, I'd had far too much and drunk it far too quickly.'

She sat for a moment and stared at her hands, still trembling slightly on her lap.

'Next morning I just didn't want to move, but Carol kept shaking me and telling me we had to go. I didn't know where or what she was talking about. I had a blinding headache and felt terribly ill.' She looked up briefly. 'A classic hangover, I suppose.

'Anyway, before I knew it, Frank was round with his estate car and they were loading it.'

'Frank kept stock here?' Gillian asked.

'Some of it. Mostly the paintings Carol copied for him, and some of the jewellery I'd made. All the things he couldn't store openly.'

All the forgeries, Gillian thought.

135

'It seems that at the party I'd been showing off a bit about our fabulous business. Frank had noticed some people were beginning to ask rather inquisitive questions—like where did we manage to find such marvellous antiques—and such an endless supply of them?'

'Of course, everyone at the party knew that you and Carol were artists!'

Holly nodded.

'So Frank decided we'd better hide the stock until he could disperse it through the country,' she continued. 'He'd discovered an old disused cottage on the far side of the moor. Some of it was still quite weatherproof. It seemed an ideal place.'

'We all had to help load his car. Chris, too.' She sighed wearily.

'Chris knew what you'd been doing?'

'No, I don't think so. Not until then. He's bright, though and he realised that something fishy was going on, when everything was being moved out of the house with such speed and with everyone in such filthy tempers.

'When Frank insisted we all got in the car I said I wanted to stay behind with Chris. Believe me, Gillian, I never wanted him involved at all.'

Holly went to her dressing-table and took the bird brooch out again and laid it on the palm of her hand.

'To be truthful, I don't think Carol really intended to involve him either. It was just that

136

he was such a super little artist, with such original ideas. You see, a design like this could come from any age, culture or country.'

'It was easy, then, to sell it as genuine antique?'

'Too easy.' Holly shrugged. 'It made money fast, and that was what Carol wanted. She'd got herself into a bit of a mess. Roy had left money behind for Chris to go to a good school and Carol had used the money to finance her art side of the business.'

'She was copying good paintings and Frank was selling those as originals,' Gillian prompted.

'Yes. She was also reproducing miniatures and silhouettes.'

'Of course, there's nothing wrong in reproducing articles,' Gillian pointed out. 'As long as they're sold as such.'

'We weren't selling reproductions, Frank sold everything as genuine antique.' Holly broke down again. 'We were thieves—worse than thieves!'

Gillian held her close, and gradually the girl regained control.

'I don't remember what happened at all after we left the cottage that day. The whole morning had been a blur to me. I only know one minute we were driving along and the next there was this terrible crash—'

'You were driving?'

'No.'

137

'Then—then how could you have killed Carol?'

'I—I was in the back with Chris. I think Carol said something that I disagreed with and I leaned forward to talk to her. Evidently, we were going round a corner and I lurched into her, knocking her hands off the wheel and we crashed.'

'What did she say to you?'

'I don't know. Frank told me, but I forget. I don't even remember what I said to her.'

There was a long silence, then Gillian said very quietly, 'You only know this is what happened because Frank told you?'

'Yes, of course. I told you, Gillian, everything was a blur.'

'You don't even remember the car going round the corner or your lurching against Carol?'

'I remember nothing,' the girl said desperately.

'And after the crash?'

'After—somehow I got Chris out of the car. I remember everything from that minute. My brain seemed to clear instantly and—and I can still see everything—everything—'

'But you got Chris out?' Gillian persisted softly.

'Yes—Carol was sort of slumped over the wheel—knocked out, I thought. There was no blood—nothing seemed to be broken, but I didn't want Chris there.'

138

She paused for a long moment.

'I told Frank I was going to the nearest phone to get an ambulance. He was absolutely furious. He wanted me to help unload the car first.'

'But Carol—'

'He was more worried about his stock,' she said bitterly.

'So what did you do?'

'I grabbed Chris's hand and ran.'

'But the house you ran to—the people there would know you'd been in an accident!'

There was a long pause.

'I ran all the way back here.'

'Here?'

'I was terrified. I suppose I just bolted for home. Chris seemed to know how I felt. We didn't want to see anyone. I phoned for an ambulance the minute I came in, but—' Holly's voice faded to a whisper '—Carol was dead when the ambulance reached them.'

*　　　*　　　*

Holly shrugged again and spoke flatly.

'They said at the hospital that she'd died instantly in the crash.' Suddenly, she put her head in her hands. 'If only I hadn't spoken to her! It was all my fault,' she sobbed.

Gently, Gillian took the girl's hands away from her face.

'The crash was an accident. You didn't kill

139

Carol. You don't know that you bumped Carol, or even that you spoke to her. Only what Frank told you. Isn't that correct?'

Holly raised her head. Her smooth ivory skin was filmed with tears, but her eyes were wide with surprise.

'Yes, but that's what happened. I couldn't remember a thing—' Her voice faltered. 'Do you think Frank was lying?'

'A strong possibility,' Gillian said dryly. 'But in any event, Holly, it was an accident. Frank has no hold over you.'

'He has. He'll tell Roy.'

'You'll tell Roy exactly what happened. Believe me, he won't blame you.'

'If I do, he'll find out about Frank—and Chris. He'd never forgive me, if he knew how we'd involved Chris in this business.'

She shook her head. 'Roy thinks Carol was alone when she crashed. I'd have to tell him Frank, Chris and I were with her. I can't say it wasn't my fault, because I don't know if that's the truth or not. No one else can say either!'

'There's Chris,' Gillian said very quietly. 'He was there.'

'You know he won't speak.'

'Not even to help you?'

'Not after what Frank said to him. He told Chris the police would arrest him for drawing the bird, and that I'd be put in prison, and his mother would be exposed as a thief. Chris is terrified of Roy finding out everything. Why do

140

you think he won't talk at all? He's afraid he'll give something away.'

Gillian felt a tide of bitterness rising inside her. Frank Reynolds had destroyed Carol, was holding Holly in a blackmailer's grip—and had terrified a young boy and shut Chris away in a silent prison of fear and guilt.

She could feel herself trembling with rage and a desire for revenge. Slowly, she straightened her cramped limbs and stood up in front of Holly.

'I'll put a stop to him, Holly. There must be a way. If there is, I'll find it.' Her voice sounded far away and detached, but there was an undertone of grim determination.

'How can you do anything without Roy finding out?'

Gillian walked over to the window. A fluttering kite riding high caught her eye. Her gaze fell. Chris was controlling the string, both hands gripping firmly.

Roy stood directly behind him, his hands ready to give some steadying support, should the wind prove too strong for Chris. They moved in unison, backs bent slightly back, legs apart, heads tilted to watch the straining kite. There was an impression of easy comradeship about father and son that seemed so natural.

Yet it had taken a long time for this achievement. Whatever she did, she must be careful not to destroy this. She knew any mention of the accident would bring all Chris's

141

terrors to the surface, and he'd withdraw again from his father.

There must be another way to find out the truth. Reluctantly, Gillian remembered her original intention. She'd tried before to question Frank's sister, Barbara, but it had looked then as if she was just taking revenge on Barbara for her relationship with James. Now there was no alternative.

'I'll speak to Barbara,' she said quietly, turning to face Holly.

She was surprised to see fresh tears in the girl's eyes.

'I'm sorry—to make you do this. I'm sorry for trying to use you, Gillian. That first day you came to the Eidelweiss I saw you talking to Barbara. I hung around deliberately, listened to your conversation.' She lowered her eyes.

'Forget it, it's over now. Anyway, how could you use me?'

'I had some crazy idea that you might help—you know, like an ally. You and me against the Reynolds.'

Gillian stared at her. She hadn't realised the girl was so desperate. 'You mean—a kind of pact?'

'Yes. I'd tried to attract your attention when you were leaving the hotel, but you didn't hear me. So I took the shortcut to the hotel's entrance road. I was so desperate I just ran out.

'I never meant to cause that accident.' She broke down again. 'I've made such a mess of things.'

'No, Holly, you haven't. You've been a victim of selfish people.'

Gently she drew the girl to her feet. 'Now, freshen-up and come downstairs. Look as natural as possible. Don't give anything away to Roy and Chris. And leave everything to me.'

For a moment, as Holly raised trusting blue eyes to hers, Gillian felt doubtful. She, Gillian Parker, the quiet mouse, the complacent, unimaginative housewife, was going to solve this enormous, evil threat?

When she went downstairs, however, and looked out of the kitchen window, she saw the man and his son, and she knew she had to do it. Frank Reynolds was ruining this family for his own ends.

She realised that Carol Andrews had been partly to blame, too, for she'd obviously been a selfish, headstrong girl, and had led the weaker Holly. How could she have involved her son, though? Gillian would never understand that.

Although she had no idea how Chris felt about his mother, she had no intention of destroying any precious memories he might hold. No matter how treacherous one person might appear to another, a mother held a special place in her child's heart forever. Gillian would never wreck that.

The only way left to her was to approach Barbara Reynolds.

She hadn't realised that she was so

143

preoccupied with the problem until she became aware later that Roy kept glancing in her direction. At last he spoke.

'Gill, is something worrying you? Is it money? Do I give you enough for the house-keeping? Or do you have too much work to do? Please tell me. Perhaps I can help.'

She turned to him and summoned a smile. They were at ease with each other now, and she was secretly moved by the natural way he called her 'Gill.' In fact, their friendship had progressed to the stage when she felt she could have discussed anything with him, even the most personal feelings—but never what was bothering her!

She knew that he, too, kept no secrets from her and that he would be puzzled and hurt if she brushed aside his offer of help. She had just told Holly to be as natural as possible with Roy, and she must do the same. It might be necessary, though, to tell a few lies to protect them.

'Thanks for the offer. The fact is, I have to face going to the Eidelweiss again.' That at least was the truth. 'I have to speak to James.'

Roy's face closed a little. 'Problems—or have you changed your mind about the divorce?'

She shook her head. 'No. The break is final, Roy. I have no regrets about that.'

His face cleared. 'Domestic and financial matters, then?'

'Something like that.'

That was no lie, either. Only Roy didn't realise it was his domestic matters which weighed so heavily on her.

After tea, Holly seemed much calmer, and the four played a quiet game of Scrabble. They were a cosy group, and it was obvious that Chris was relaxed and content. He no longer seemed so scared, so wary of everyone.

As she watched him painstakingly set out a word on the board, she wondered if she was making a mistake. Perhaps Chris would talk again, anyway, even without the threat of Frank removed.

Then she glanced at Holly who, despite her laughs and smiles tonight, still had smudges under her eyes. No, Frank had to go.

*　　*　　*

Next morning, about ten-thirty, she set off for the hotel. She judged it to be a good time to catch Barbara, hoping the reception desk would be quiet.

All night Gillian had been struggling with the best way to put the whole business to the girl. She didn't want Barbara to think that she had any spiteful motive, only that she had the best interests of the Andrews' family at heart.

The first set-back was when she found a stranger behind the reception desk.

'Miss Reynolds is ill today,' the girl told her.

145

'If it's a personal matter, you could call at the staff bungalow.'

To her surprise, she found James at the bungalow, but not Barbara.

He was both distraught and embarrassed.

'She's in hospital, Gillian. She went yesterday for her usual monthly check-up and they kept her in. Blood pressure problems. Is that bad, do you think?'

Gillian smothered a wry smile at James's concern. He'd had little for her over the last few months. But then, that was past and gone.

'I shouldn't think it's too serious. Anyway, she couldn't be in better hands. Can I sit down for a moment?'

Without waiting for a reply, she sank into a chair.

She could hardly go to the hospital and confront Barbara with her brother's fraudulent activities. The subject was too potentially emotional and would be bad for her if she wasn't well.

'Actually, I'm glad you called,' James said quickly. 'I'd been hoping to see you. Our ... the house has been sold, but I can't give an entry date until you ... er, remove your bits and pieces.'

'I'll go down to Banford as soon as I can and collect the rest of my clothes.'

'Do you think ... I mean would you mind ... could you perhaps pack up the stuff I've left there and bring it back with you? You are

146

coming back to Harbury?'

Gillian almost laughed out loud. Really, James was preposterous. Here they were, in the process of obtaining a divorce, and he still wasn't able to cope with handling things on his own.

'Yes.' She sighed. 'I'll bring your things back with me.' Her tone became brisk. 'In return, you can do something for me.'

Maybe she couldn't go to the hospital and question Barbara, but there was nothing to stop James asking her a few questions about Frank.

'I have a problem, James. It's the Andrews family. Or rather what Frank Reynolds has done, and is doing, to them.'

James's plump face puckered with resentment.

'This has nothing whatsoever to do with Barbara and you,' she said quickly.

'I'm happy for you both. I've no wish to cause you any distress, particularly now with the baby coming, but I think you ought to know about Frank. After all, I would never have known anything about this if I hadn't had to come up here to see you in the first place.'

Briefly and concisely she told him about the faking of the antiques, the involvement with Carol Andrews, her death, and the blackmailing of Holly.

'Perhaps worst of all, Frank has so terrified Roy's son that he hasn't spoken a word since

147

the day of the accident.'

James said nothing for a moment or two, then he shook his head.

'That's terrible, really terrible. I've honestly never really taken to the fellow, but I can't believe he'd do all that.'

'Well, he has,' she said flatly. 'I want you to ask Barbara where Frank was on the day of the accident.'

'M'm, yes, I will—as soon as she's better.'

'No, James, you must ask her now! This has gone on long enough. Barbara is the only person I can think of who will be able to get at the truth without suffering at Frank's hands.'

'Oh, come now, Gillian, that's a bit dramatic—'

'You do realise she's been selling Frank's faked antiques here in the hotel?'

James paled. 'I hadn't thought about that. I'll see nothing is sold from now on. But I'm not telling her anything until she's better,' he finished stubbornly.

Gillian blew up. 'You and Barbara are about to have a child. Would you like him to suffer the way Chris Andrews is?'

James turned on her. 'That's unfair. You're jealous of Barbara because we didn't have any—'

'Oh, for heaven's sake. Don't be so childish, James. I am not jealous. I only care about Roy and Chris and Holly!'

She saw the surprise and enlightenment on

148

James's face, and the full meaning of what she'd said came home to her.

Roy, Chris, and Holly were the people she cared about. The truth had been surprised out of her. Something that she hadn't admitted to herself, that she loved them—all three.

Wryly, she remembered Sue, her neighbour in Banford, warning her not to get involved. Well, she had, but they weren't substitutes for James any longer. She truly loved them.

'I'll mention it to Barbara.'

'Thanks.'

'When I think it won't upset her too much.'

Gillian repeated her thanks with all the sarcasm she could muster. James hadn't changed one bit. Still the same old, dithering, indecisive person he'd always been.

She was too disgusted even to slam the door as she left the bungalow. She was on her own now. Entirely. It could take James days to approach Barbara on the subject.

Gillian had a strange sensation of urgency. Somehow, she felt Holly was on the verge of a breakdown with Frank's ever-increasing threats.

She knew, too, that if Holly did break down, Chris would be badly affected. He was an intelligent boy for nine, and he must know Holly was still suffering and afraid. He would realise the threat was still there.

One thing was vital to her now—the return of her car. She went to Harbury Garage straight from the Eidelweiss.

The mechanic was cautious.

'We've patched her up, Mrs Parker, but I'm none too happy. Must you have her right away?'

'Yes, I must.'

'Don't worry, I'll take the responsibility. As long as brakes and steering are O K!'

'Sure, everything's O K. I'm just not sure how long the engine will last. Don't push her too hard, no faster than forty. Remember, she's been knocked about.'

'I'll treat her like a convalescent,' she assured him.

* * *

She discussed her visit to Banford with Roy, and it was decided she'd go on Friday and return on the Sunday.

'I'd like to come and help, but I guess this is something you have to do alone,' he said.

'Yes, this is the final link. When I come back, I'll be finished with that life altogether.'

'Ready to start a new one,' Roy said warmly.

Friday was wet, dreary. She'd told Roy she was going to take it slowly to Banford. She didn't tell him the reason.

The motorway was not for her on this trip. Her route was through every single town that lay between Harbury and Banford. Her objective—every antique shop she could find.

She'd persuaded Holly to give her a list of all the items she'd made for Frank, with a full description and the marks she put on the silver jewellery and ornaments. She also had a list of the major paintings Carol had copied. She didn't bother with the miniatures and silhouettes. They would be almost impossible to trace.

At each shop she visited, she repeated a story she'd made up about trying to trace family heirlooms which her brother had sold to Skua Antiques and which she was now trying to buy back.

It was a long and arduous day. Most of the items, which the shopkeepers had bought from Frank, had been resold, and she had to pretend dismay.

Each call brought more proof, however. The farther she travelled from Harbury the more items she discovered. Oh, Frank had been clever. He hadn't duplicated anything in the same town.

Her neighbour, Sue Jackson, was waiting for her at Banford. Together they emptied drawers and wardrobes. As Gillian flung clothes into suitcases, she poured out the whole story to her friend.

'When you have enough proof, will you show it to this Frank Reynolds?' Sue asked.

'Yes. I have a list of all the shops who've bought from him, and I wouldn't hesitate to inform them of what he's been doing.'

151

'You're taking a risk with someone like him.'

'Yes, but it's blackmail, too,' Gillian said coolly. 'The only thing a man like him understands. It's my only weapon and I mean to win!'

She could see admiration, mixed with caution, in Sue's eyes.

Gillian grinned. 'You didn't think I had it in me.'

'Well, I—' Sue paused. 'I guess you just have a powerful driving force this time.'

'I only want two things from Frank Reynolds. One, that he should stop selling reproductions as genuine antiques immediately, particularly those made by Carol and Holly. Two, that he tells Holly she didn't kill Carol.'

'What about Chris?'

'I don't want him near Chris. I don't even want Chris to see him.

'Once Frank has gone, Holly can tell Chris that the danger is over. That will be enough, I'm sure. Chris will then begin to talk again.'

* * *

Next day, Sue took Gillian to the Horseshoe Antique shop in Banford. The owner was a friend of Sue's and had examined the silver bangle that Gillian had sent.

Now Gillian told him in confidence about the forgeries.

152

'Right, lady,' Mr Bishop said. 'We have our own method of dealing with the likes of him. Just leave it to me.'

'It's a bit more complicated than that. I'm trying to protect someone else,' Gillian said.

'The forger?' he asked shrewdly.

Gillian hesitated.

'Working under duress. I suppose it's blackmail?' he said succinctly.

She nodded. Mr Bishop was no fool.

'I'd rather you did nothing just yet—until I've had a chance to speak to the man.'

He shrugged. 'O K. But I certainly wouldn't touch another thing from Skua Antiques.'

Gillian spent that night at Sue's house, feeling elated and confident. She was sure now she could stop Frank blackmailing Holly. She had plenty of hard facts about his sales.

At the same time, she realised she was walking a tightrope. She didn't want Frank to expose the parts Holly and Carol had played in the business. He needed careful handling.

She drove straight back to Harbury on the Sunday night. It was a very dark night but she felt excited and happy, like someone returning home with good news. She'd have to keep this to herself for a bit, though.

Roy's cottage was at the end of a winding lane, sheltered by hedgerows and trees. She was about to turn into the drive when a dark figure stepped out suddenly in front of the car and Gillian instinctively slammed on the

153

brakes. The car shuddered to a halt and stalled. Gillian's heart was pounding with fright. She'd only just managed to stop.

Before she had a chance to get out of her car, though, the figure thrust an arm through the open window, and Gillian felt the cold steel of a knife at her throat. To her horror, she realised it was Frank Reynolds.

'Don't make a sound,' he hissed.

As he unlocked the rear door and climbed in, Gillian could feel his breath on the back of her neck.

'Start up the car and turn it out of the drive. Don't try anything.'

Her hand trembling, Gillian started up the car. Again, she felt the knife touch her neck.

'Drive away as slowly and quietly as you've ever done.'

Gillian involuntarily glanced into the cottage. Chris was there, in his bedroom, watching from his window. He looked frightened and confused.

She opened her mouth, but before a sound escaped, Frank's hand was clamped over it.

'Drive now!' he hissed. The blade pricked her skin.

She released the handbrake and the car moved off, but through her still-open window she heard a sound. A voice.

A voice she'd never heard before.

'Daddy! Daddy! Come quickly! Daddy!'

Chris Andrews was speaking!

CHAPTER EIGHT

The blade of the knife was cold and menacing on Gillian's neck. She could feel Frank Reynolds' breath on her cheek as he leaned over the back of her seat and gave instructions.

'Turn on to the main road and go south.' He spoke into her ear. 'No fancy signals, like flashing lights, to warn other drivers. I can see everything you're doing.'

Strangely, Gillian was quite calm. Her fear had vanished when she heard Chris Andrews speak.

She felt only contempt for the man who'd kidnapped her. While he was armed, she would do exactly as he said. But, at the same time, she planned to escape at the first opportunity. Frank Reynolds was a petty criminal, a blackmailer, a parasite in society. Surely she could outwit him!

They were approaching the moors. Still she said nothing.

She realised Frank must be directing her towards the old, deserted cottage which Holly had told her about. She tried to remember everything the girl had said. She wanted to be prepared as much as possible.

She knew one room of the cottage was secure. It was the hiding place for Frank's faked antiques. But was the rest of the place

155

still standing? Was it far from the main road?

To escape, she would need her car. Therefore she must immobilise Frank somehow. Lock him up or knock him out.

Gillian smiled grimly to herself. She was quite calmly planning to hurt another human being—she, who didn't believe in violence!

This was different, though. Other people were involved. Frank had to be stopped now before he could blackmail Holly any longer or continue to frighten Chris.

'Just keep going, my pretty lady,' the voice purred from the back seat.

'Pretty and clever, aren't you? Checking on all those antique shops to find out what I'd sold. Lucky I have friends in the trade with good noses for spies, isn't it?'

'You mean there are more of your kind?' she said tersely.

'Watch it,' Frank's voice rasped. 'This knife might slip.

'Oh, I wouldn't cut you badly enough to stop your driving, but a nasty cut on your cheek would spoil your pretty face. Now stop talking and drive. Fast.'

As she put her foot down on the accelerator she glanced quickly in the mirror. She'd been hoping that Chris had seen what happened. Even if he had, would he—or could he—tell Roy what he'd seen? She'd been desperately hoping that someone would be following. She looked again. The road behind was

156

totally empty.

Suddenly, Frank laughed.

'Who do you keep looking for—the Seventh Cavalry? Nobody's going to come to your rescue. Oh, no, lady, I planned this as one of my better jobs.'

The knife moved away as he eased back in his seat with self-satisfaction.

'I found out quite easily from your ex-husband that you'd gone to Banford for the week-end. I'd already guessed as much from the information I'd received from my friends. So all I did was wait for you to come back. The Andrews didn't even know I was hiding at the bottom of their garden.'

The road began to twist and turn as it climbed over the hills. Approaching a corner too fast, Gillian pressed her foot on the brake pedal. It was soft, sluggish. She caught her breath.

'Easy!' Frank leaned forward again. 'I know your game. You'll run the car off the road and make a dash for it. Forget that. Keep going.'

'I wasn't going to do anything. It—' The steel blade of the knife was cold against her skin.

'Shut up and drive on—but carefully.'

She clamped her lips together. She'd been going to tell him about the brakes. The garage mechanic had warned her to treat the car gently and never to drive at the speed Frank Reynolds insisted on.

'Over the next rise, you'll see a cart track on your left. Take it,' he instructed.

Gillian topped the rise, then slowed the car by changing into a lower gear.

The track was littered with stones and they hiccuped along. Just round the shoulder of a rocky outcrop she came on the cottage, neatly hidden from the main road. By now, she was going so slowly that she was able to stop easily.

'Now, reverse the car and park it along the side of the cottage.'

Gillian did so, realising that even if someone did approach the cottage, they would not see her car.

'Right, Mrs Parker, switch off.' His hand reached over. 'I'll have the keys. Out!'

Gillian's mind was working furiously. She tried to take note of the geography of the surrounding countryside, to see if there was a quicker route to the main road. She knew that, when she made her break, she must know exactly where she was going and not run wildly in the wrong direction.

Frank Reynolds pushed her from behind.

'People get lost in these hills. Bodies have been found months after folk disappeared. Don't chance it.'

The cottage had four standing walls, but little roof, except over one corner. This must be the weatherproof room Holly had spoken of.

For the first time, she thought seriously about what Frank Reynolds was planning.

158

Was he going to leave her imprisoned here—or use her as a hostage?

She turned round to face him. 'Why have you brought me here?'

'You're going to work for me for a bit, lady. You've finished me here, so I'm clearing out. But I'm going to make you pay for that.

'Now get in there.' He pushed her towards the gaping hole that had been the cottage's front door.

* * *

She had to escape now—or never!

She threw herself back against Frank. As he reeled away, she sprang forward to run.

At once she realised she hadn't thrown him off balance, as she'd hoped. His reactions were amazingly fast. He spread his arms wide, knife in one hand, and danced from side to side like a boxer, effectively keeping between her and the car. There was no way she could dodge past him.

She whirled and ran into the cottage. Beams hung drunkenly from rotten rafters. The earthen floor was tufted with coarse moor grass. Weeds were everywhere, and a small tree had taken root in the yawning grate.

The remains of a shelf leaned against a corner, rusted nails protruding from the wood. In a flash, Gillian grabbed it. She had a weapon!

159

She swung wildly towards Frank. Amazingly, the wood caught his wrist, and the force of her swing knocked the knife from his hand.

He turned his head to look for it, and she started from the corner towards the gaping doorway.

He was faster. He leaped up, caught one of the hanging beams, and sent it crashing down in the path of her flight. It caught her squarely on her shin.

With a scream of pain, Gillian toppled over and landed face down in the scrubby grass.

Frank Reynolds bent down and, grabbing her by her arm, dragged her upright.

'My leg,' she shrieked, blinded with pain. 'I can't walk, I can't stand.'

'You haven't far to go,' he grunted, and dragged her towards the only door in the derelict cottage.

She heard him fumbling with a key and padlock, and then she was hauled into the room and flung on to a spoon-back Victorian chair. She huddled there, both hands gripping her useless and agonising leg.

'Serves you right,' Frank said viciously. 'I knew you'd try something. Waste of time. You've just hurt yourself for nothing.'

He strode over to a tall, rosewood chest in the corner of the room.

'You're no use to me now. I'll have to pack it all myself. But just look at these.' He spilled a drawer full of rings and brooches at Gillian's feet.

'And those.' Another drawer was full of napkin rings, bracelets, shoe horns, button hooks, embroidery scissors, and all the little ornaments the Victorians had been so fond of.

'A fortune in antiques here—made by Miss Holly Andrews.'

He whirled round and pulled away a pile of old rugs to reveal a stack of pictures—watercolours, oils, and line drawings.

'More gen-u-ine antiques for my new customers over the Atlantic. I've fooled them here long enough. Now I'll go and start on the Yanks.'

He held up a picture right in front of Gillian. 'This is painted by the famous Old Master—Carol Andrews.' He laughed in her face.

He began to gather the pictures together. 'Now, Carol was a girl after my own heart. She liked to live dangerously. This game was fun to her.'

'That's why you do it?' Gillian said.

He shrugged. 'For the money and for the kicks.'

'You care about no one, do you? Not Holly, not Chris. Did you even care for Carol?'

His face was dark with an emotion Gillian didn't understand.

'She was useful to me.'

'You don't care that she's dead!'

'She was a lousy driver and she took a

chance.'

'So Holly didn't cause the accident?'

Frank laughed derisively. 'That stupid kid would believe anything, especially with a hangover. I just put the frighteners on her.'

'You're despicable. Holly's terrified of you and so is Chris.'

He ignored her.

'What about your sister?' she asked.

'Barbara? She's a pain in the neck. I won't miss her, and she won't miss me.'

'You won't get any more paintings, anyway,' she pointed out.

'I'll find someone else. No sweat.' He turned and looked at her, his eyes smiling cruelly. 'And, of course, I'll have a regular supply of silver.'

'Not any longer,' Gillian snapped at him. 'I'm going to tell Roy Andrews the full story.'

'You're not going to get the chance,' he said, quite flatly.

Gillian tried to get up, but the pain seemed to slice through her whole leg. She couldn't even sink back in the chair easily. The slightest movement was pure agony.

Did it matter? It seemed Frank's intention was quite clear. He was going to put her out of reach of the Andrews family for good.

She looked at him through eyes almost closed with pain. He was just a smalltime criminal surely? A petty thief. Was he really capable of murder?

162

He moved between the store of jewellery and paintings and her car, methodically packing and loading. Finally, he stood before her, empty handed.

'You've been of great assistance,' he said sarcastically. 'I don't even need to tie you up. You can't possibly move anywhere with that leg. Screaming is a waste of effort, too.'

'You can't leave me here. It could be days before anyone comes.'

'Exactly. Sweet dreams, Mrs P.'

Swiftly, he left the room and she heard him fixing the padlock outside. Then she heard the car engine running.

Dimly, through her ever-increasing pain, she remembered there was something she'd been going to tell him about the car. What was it? She couldn't remember now. If only her brain was clear.

The thought was interrupted as the glass in the small window of the room suddenly shattered. She looked at the gaping hole and heard Frank's voice.

'Just a little insurance!' He laughed loudly.

A burning rag landed at her feet. Her scream was drowned out by the roar of her car.

Frank Reynolds had left her immobilised in a burning room!

The rag had landed near her left foot, but it was her left leg which she'd injured and she couldn't move it at all.

Gritting her teeth, she tried to twist her body

round so that her right foot could stamp on the rag and extinguish the flame. Pain and nausea swept over her and she knew she was on the verge of fainting.

She tried to stay low to breathe some air. The room was filled with heavy smoke, but she was still getting some fresh air from the gap under the door. But for how long?

Panic rose inside her. She was trapped, doomed to die in this room because of Frank Reynolds.

He'd got away, scot-free. Holly was still carrying the burden of guilt over Carol's death. She could still be blackmailed by Frank. And Chris? How long would his recovery last if Frank was still on the loose?

The thought, too, that she might never see Roy Andrews again gave Gillian an inner pain, as anguishing as that from her leg.

Frank Reynolds would not win!

She propelled herself along the floor using her elbows, trying to shield her nose and mouth with her forearm. Frank had discarded the old rugs which had covered the paintings. Stretching out, she caught a fringe with her fingertips and slowly, painstakingly, dragged the rug towards her.

The constant pain now affecting her whole body made every action seem like a slow-motion replay on television. She inched the rug towards her and, with a weak twist of her wrist, jerked it in the direction of the smoking rag. It covered it, but didn't quite douse the smoke.

Oh, Roy, please help me. I need you now, she prayed soundlessly.

She moved on towards the window, more painful inches, more racking coughs. Chris, why didn't you see me? she asked herself, coughing in the swirling smoke.

The Victorian chair, with its long 'skirt' hiding the curved legs, was now smouldering. She must get out. She must reach Roy, Chris and Holly.

As she urged her body along the floor, she kept her mind fixed on those loved ones rather than the menace of the fire. So intense was her concentration that she could hear their voices in her head.

* * *

'Daddy! Daddy! Find Gillian.'

'I will, Chris. If she's here, we'll find her.'

Then there was a steady thumping noise. Gillian crawled on.

'Gillian! Gillian! Are you there?'

Her eyes were blurred, her concentration upset. She turned her head.

The thumping continued. Straining through the smoke she saw the door. It was shaking. There was someone outside. It had to be Roy!

'The window! Roy, the window!' Her throat was constricted with smoke.

But he had heard. Within seconds, he was at

the gap where the window had been.

'Gillian! Oh, my God. Chris, stand clear.'

Through the hazy smoke, Gillian saw Roy tear off his anorak and wrap it round his hand. With a huge, nylon-padded fist, he wrenched at the windowframe. Rusted hinges, rotting wood, gave under his pressure and the whole structure came away and crashed on the ground outside.

He climbed through the gap and made for Gillian and cradled her in his arms.

'My leg—I can't move at all.'

'I'll put out the fire first,' he said, and dragged the remaining rugs over the smouldering furniture.

'Chris,' he shouted. 'Get the first-aid box from the car.'

He then approached the door, lifted his foot, and smashed it open.

Fresh air rushed in, sending the remaining smoke billowing up to the roof.

Roy knelt beside her and, through the blur of her pain, she saw that he, too, was near breaking point. He took off his sweater and pillowed it under her head, holding her close as he did so.

'Thank God we got here in time,' he murmured, and his lips touched her forehead. The love and comfort of that brief kiss penetrated Gillian's pain, giving her a peace she hadn't known for many months.

Chris ran in with the first-aid box, his eyes

166

wide with horror and concern.

'Hi, Chris,' she whispered.

'Are you going to be all right?' The words rushed out. 'Gillian, are you?'

She nodded. 'I'll be fine. I just wanted to hear you say my name.'

She felt Roy's hands gently straightening her leg, and slowly she slid into unconsciousness.

The next few hours were mercifully hazy to Gillian.

Fleeting spells of consciousness showed her that she'd been put in the back of the car, with Chris beside her. Holly was there, too, sitting in the front passenger seat, but smiling encouragingly whenever Gillian opened her eyes.

She was aware, too, that Roy was driving slowly and carefully, trying to avoid the slightest jolt of the car.

Next time she opened her eyes she caught glimpses of white, and there was a cool atmosphere. She realised she was in hospital. X-rays and sleep followed, but she was soon allowed home.

Next morning, she awoke to the sound of birdsong from the garden. The sun was doing its best to slide through the gap in the curtains, and she gingerly pulled herself upright. She knew she must be much better—she was starving!

She could hear the rattle of cups and the chatter of voices from downstairs. Chatter—in this house? It was wonderful—a miracle.

The approaching voices became louder, then were suddenly hushed as her door was slowly pushed open.

'Good morning!' she sang out.

'She's awake!' The door swung wide, and Chris rushed in, followed by Roy.

Breakfast was a cheerful, chattering affair, but eventually Roy sent Chris off with the empty tray.

'You've no idea how glad I am to see you so well,' Roy said, looking at her from the door as he closed it behind Chris.

'You've no idea how glad I am to be here,' she said softly. 'There were moments when I wondered if I would ever see you all again.'

He walked over to the bed and sat in the chair beside it. It seemed quite natural when he reached out and took her hand and held it in his.

'Don't think of that ever again.'

She smiled ruefully. 'Believe me, I don't want to. But I must know how you found me. Did Chris see Frank force me to drive away?'

'No. He'd been sitting up in his room looking for you for about an hour, then he came rushing down ... calling me.'

Roy stopped for a moment. 'At first, I was so shaken by hearing him speak that I didn't take any notice of what he was saying. Then, gradually, I realised he was talking about you. He said you'd driven off with someone in your

168

car, and that you hadn't even looked in.' He paused and shook his head.

'Chris was so excited that I thought he'd been mistaken. Then I thought that perhaps you'd decided to go straight to the Eidelweiss with James's things. Chris wasn't happy with that. I think he thought you weren't coming back.'

Roy pressed her hand.

'I realise now that he must have known something was wrong and the urgency of the situation had brought back his speech. If only I'd listened to him—'

Gillian returned the pressure of his hand. 'It's over now. But what made you come after me?'

'James came to see me.'

'James?' Gillian was astounded.

'Yes. He was worried about you.'

'Me?'

Roy smiled. 'Yes, he was. People do care about you, my dear.

'He told me all you'd said about Frank and that he was worried he hadn't done anything about it. Evidently, on Saturday, Frank had questioned him about you. He thought nothing of it at the time, since you were in Banford. Then he began to realise you were at risk there—and he'd told Frank exactly where you were. And this really worried him—he hadn't seen Frank since then.'

169

'James came here to tell you all this?' Gillian asked.

'He came to see if you'd returned.' Roy's expression changed.

'Suddenly, Chris's claim of someone in your car became quite frightening. Holly flew into an instant panic, and it was then I realised that something very dangerous had been going on.'

'So you came to the cottage?'

He nodded. 'Holly said if it was Frank in your car, he would take you there.'

There was a long pause.

'I'll never forget what you did and what you risked for us,' Roy said huskily.

'You would have done the same, had you known,' she told him softly.

'Grateful is such an inadequate word to express my feelings and it's only one aspect of—' Roy paused, ruffled his hair with frustration.

'Words aren't my talent, Gillian. Bridges are. If I could build a bridge to show you how I care about you, it would be beautiful, magnificent, everlasting—'

Roy slowly raised her hand to his cheek and held it there. That and the expression in his eyes were more binding than paragraphs of words.

*　　*　　*

Gradually, over the next few days, Gillian regained her strength and her leg slowly

170

mended.

By gentle questioning on her part, she discovered that Roy knew the whole story of Frank, Carol, and Holly. She didn't know what had been said between them, and it must have been painful to all, but it was over now and should be buried for ever.

Chris was now totally happy, talkative, and obviously adored his father.

'Daddy said it was all right about drawing the bird,' Chris told her. 'I didn't do anything wrong at all. And he thinks I'm good at drawing.

'I said I wanted to draw you a picture 'cos— 'cos, well, I like you, Gillian. I didn't know what you'd like, but Daddy said a bridge. So I did. Here it is. Why do you like bridges, Gillian?'

'They mean something very special to me, Chris,' she told him with a tender smile.

Gillian had wasted no time in setting Holly's mind at ease. She told her exactly what Frank had said about the accident.

'So I didn't kill Carol after all.' Holly sat quite still, staring at her hands in her lap. 'That's all I care about. I feel I can go on living now.'

Then the time came when Gillian had to ask about Frank.

'He seems to have vanished,' Roy told her.

'You know I only remembered a few days ago that my car brakes were wonky,' she said.

'I tried to tell Frank, but he wouldn't listen.'

'Don't think about it. You have nothing to blame yourself for.'

'Frank has all the silver and paintings in the car. If it's found, will Holly be in trouble?'

He shook his head.

'Once I knew the whole story, Holly wanted to confess her part to the police. We had a word with the local inspector.'

Roy smiled reassuringly. 'There will be no trouble for her. She was making reproductions. It was Frank who was selling them as genuine antiques.'

'Thank goodness. I don't think Holly could take much more.'

Gillian paid one more visit to the Eidelweiss Hotel. All the items she'd brought from Banford had disappeared in her car with Frank. She apologised to James.

'Goodbye, James.' Gillian shook his hand with affection. He was, basically, a nice man, but she knew she'd never really loved him enough. Nothing like the way she loved Roy.

The police inspector called a few days later. A local farmer had found skid marks on his land bordering the moor. The marks ran down into a deep tarn.

The inspector told them divers had searched, but so far hadn't discovered a body. There was only a small car, painted vivid green, which as yet they'd failed to raise.

'It must be my car,' Gillian told the

172

inspector. 'The brakes were faulty and the car was unreliable at high speeds. He didn't give me a chance to tell him.'

'You have nothing to blame yourself for, Mrs Parker,' he told her. 'He must have been taking a short cut over the moors when the car went out of control.'

On the same day, Gillian received a letter from Mr Hunter, her ex-boss in Banford. Their visit to Italy was all fixed and they would like to ask Holly to accompany them. The Hunters said they felt Gillian might prefer to stay in Harbury.

Gillian smiled when she read the letter. Mr Hunter had always been very observant where she was concerned. He must have seen how she felt about the Andrews, especially Roy, when he'd called several weeks ago.

'I think a trip to Italy is just what Holly is needing,' Gillian told Roy, after showing him the letter.

'She should get away from here for a while, forget the past year and take a fresh look at art. She is talented. The Hunters will make a fuss of her; she needs that, too.'

Roy was happy to agree with her, and Holly was overjoyed. The Hunters arrived two weeks later to fetch her.

As they stood by the car, Holly kissed Roy and Chris. Then she turned to Gillian and took her hands.

'You will be here when I come back?' she

asked anxiously.

'Of course she will. Gillian's never going away again,' Chris said.

He smiled at Gillian. 'I don't want you to leave.'

He turned to his father. 'You don't want her to leave, do you, Daddy?'

'No, I don't,' Roy said, not taking his eyes from Gillian.

'And you don't want to leave, Gillian?' the boy demanded.

'No, I don't,' she echoed Roy.

They weren't words of love, but there was plenty of time now for that. Time to say a thousand words.

After Holly had left with the Hunters, the three of them went out into the quiet countryside. Chris and the dog raced around them, but even then they didn't talk. They didn't have the opportunity.

'Why do seagulls scream, Daddy?'

'When does a tree know to stop growing, Gillian?'

'Can we all go to an adventure park for our holidays?'

'I'll teach Gillian to swing on a tree rope. I expect you know how to do it, Daddy.'

'Can we do—'

Roy and Gillian walked behind Chris, their arms linked closely together, listening, laughing, smiling.

The once-silent Chris talked on and on, like

a brook babbling over a thousand stones, like a non-stop record, like a typewriter spilling out an endless story!

Or, like music to their ears.